# Village Fêtes Can Be Murder

Book 1

A Saffron Weald Mystery Series

By

# Ann Sutton

**An old mystery, a murdered stranger and a notebook full of secrets turn a quaint village upside down with fear and suspicion.**

At the reading of their mother's will, the lives of twin sisters Imogen and Ophelia are changed forever. In addition to leaving them the family home in the quaint village of Saffron Weald, their mother's last request is that they retire together in the cottage, Badger's Hollow. Ophelia, a retired musician, and Imogen, a recently widowed mother of two grown children, jump at the chance since they are still in good health.

Their arrival coincides with the annual village fete, and they readily agree to lend a hand with the tug of war. However, when they go to the supply tent to retrieve the rope, they discover the body of a visiting young journalist. Before the arrival of the hapless village constable, the sisters scour the murder scene and discover several clues including a notebook in the girl's bag filled with detailed notes on the villagers including one that hits shockingly close to home. Intrigued, the discovery propels them into investigating the murder themselves, taking them on a journey fraught with suspicion, startling revelations, and danger.

Will the sisters succeed in bringing the ruthless murderer to justice or will they become victims of a predator desperate to keep their dark secrets hidden? Join these delightful and amusing elderly sleuths on their first detecting adventure and meet a whole cast of colorful and quirky characters.

Fans of Agatha Christie's Miss Marple will fall in love with the smart and sassy sisters in this delightful new series.

©2024 Ann Sutton

No part of this book may be reproduced in any form whatsoever, whether by graphic, visual, electronic, film, microfilm, tape recording or any other means, without the prior written permission of the author and publisher, except in case of brief critical reviews.

This is a work of fiction. The characters, names, incidents, places and dialogue are products of the author's imagination and are not to be construed as real. The opinions and views expressed herein belong solely to the author.

Permission for the use of sources, graphics and photos is the responsibility of the author.

Published by

    Wild Poppy Publishing LLC
    Highland, UT 84003


Distributed by Wild Poppy Publishing


Cover design by Julie Matern
Cover Design ©2024 Wild Poppy Publishing LLC

Dedicated to Duchess

## Style Note

I am a naturalized American citizen born and raised in the United Kingdom. I have readers in America, the UK, Australia, Canada and beyond. But my book is set in the United Kingdom.

So which version of English should I choose?

I chose American English as it is my biggest audience, my family learns this English and my editor suggested it was the most logical.

This leads to criticism from those in other English-speaking countries, but I have neither the time nor the resources to do a special edition for each country.

I do use British words, phrases and idioms whenever I can (unless my editor does not understand them and then it behooves me to change it so that it is not confusing to my readers).

# Cast of Main Characters for Village Fêtes Can Be Murder

Ophelia Harrington - Twin sister of Imogen Pettigrew
Imogen Pettigrew - Widowed twin sister of Ophelia
Beatrice Harrington - The twins' deceased mother

*Saffron Weald Residents*
Constance 'Connie' Featherstone - Village librarian, old school friend of twins
Reginald 'Reggie' Tumblethorn - Village grocer
Harold and Harriet Cleaver - Village butchers
Peter Cleaver - Decorator
Malcolm Cleaver - Gardener
Midred Chumbley - Gossip, head bell ringer, President of WI
Arabella and Fred Fudgeford - Village sweet shop owners
Archie and Alice Puddingfield - Village bakers
Pierre Ancien - Village antique dealer
Reverend Cresswell - Vicar
Prudence Cresswell - Vicar's wife
Colonel Winstanley - Head of village Council
Lila Winterbourne aka Willa Medford - Outsider journalist
Lord Stirling - Lord of the manor
Constable Hargrove - Local Bobby
Dr. Pemberton - County doctor
Inspector Southam - County police Inspector
Tiny - Alsatian dog

*Saffron Weald Stores*
Tumblethorn's - Grocer

The Jolly Lolly - Confectioner
The Golden Crust - Baker
Cleaver's - Butcher
Pierre's Antiques Emporium - Antique shop

## Table of Contents

Prologue ..................................................................................1
Chapter 1 ................................................................................3
Chapter 2 ................................................................................9
Chapter 3 ..............................................................................17
Chapter 4 ..............................................................................23
Chapter 5 ..............................................................................28
Chapter 6 ..............................................................................37
Chapter 7 ..............................................................................44
Chapter 8 ..............................................................................49
Chapter 9 ..............................................................................54
Chapter 10 ............................................................................61
Chapter 11 ............................................................................67
Chapter 12 ............................................................................76
Chapter 13 ............................................................................86
Chapter 14 ............................................................................90
Chapter 15 ............................................................................97
Chapter 16 ..........................................................................102
Chapter 17 ..........................................................................108
Chapter 18 ..........................................................................115
Chapter 19 ..........................................................................124
Chapter 20 ..........................................................................131
Chapter 21 ..........................................................................139
Chapter 22 ..........................................................................144
Chapter 23 ..........................................................................152

Chapter 24 ................................................................... 159
Chapter 25 ................................................................... 165
Chapter 26 ................................................................... 171
Chapter 27 ................................................................... 177
Chapter 28 ................................................................... 184
The End ....................................................................... 187
About the Author ....................................................... 192

# Prologue
## Hampshire, 1928

The ticking of the antique clock was like a scar on the heavy silence in the musty solicitor's office. The toad-like lawyer peered at the elderly, identical twin sisters over wire rimmed spectacles as he sat behind his enormous, claw-footed desk. Had a fly appeared, Ophelia Harrington had no doubt a long, red tongue would dart out to snag it.

In slow motion, he rustled open the parchment paper that contained their mother's will.

*"To my beloved daughters, Imogen and Ophelia, I bequeath their childhood home, Badger's Hollow."* The deep base rumbled through Imogen's chest, the voice perfectly matching the broad, plump face and bulging eyes.

The toad coughed twice. "There is a codicil added a few months ago. *And it is my wish that my daughters live together in the cottage."*

The room erupted.

"But I thought you were coming to live with us, Mummy," protested Imogen's married daughter, Penelope.

"And *we* were hoping you would at least live close to *us*," complained Fergus, her civil servant son.

Ophelia turned in her seat. "What do you say, Imogen? Personally, I'm all for it. I'm more than ready for a change."

Imogen ran thin fingers down her long pearls. "Since Wilfred died, I *have* felt the urge to shake things up a bit," she admitted. "Our old, rambling house is far too big for me." She turned to her daughter. "I *have* considered your offer, lovey, but that was before this one was presented to me. At some point, when I become really decrepit, I shall have to force myself on you or Fergus. But until then…"

She faced her sister, a mirror image of herself. "I think it might be fun and it *is* mother's wish."

"That's settled then," declared Ophelia, rubbing her hands together. "You and I shall live in Badger's Hollow and bathe in nostalgia together."

# Chapter 1

Ophelia and Imogen stood arm in arm outside their family's slightly distressed, Elizabethan cottage. Bluebirds and red-breasted chaffinches welcomed the sisters' return with pretty birdsong from the pinnacle of the gently sloping, thatched roof.

"That's a good omen," remarked Imogen fingering the gold locket at her neck.

"Shall we?" asked Ophelia, clutching her violin case in one hand as she entered the dogwood rose arbor that framed the peeling, white gate. She reached with the other hand to open the latch.

The whitewashed walls of the little cottage were almost completely lost under the centuries-old, clinging ivy that had penetrated the black timbers with its roots. The hot July sun reflected sharply from diamond-shaped, leaded glass windows. Imogen shaded her eyes.

"Looks like we need to do some weeding," commented Ophelia as they ambled up the uneven stone path passing colorful, overgrown flower beds on each side.

Imogen reached out to touch the soft leaves of flowering shrubs. "Let's not go inside just yet, lovey. I want to visit the garden."

The proud, old cottage sat in the middle of a full acre of land that boasted a bubbling stream on its farthest border. An ancient, drooping willow dominated one side of the lawn and Imogen walked eagerly over to examine the state of the beloved, wooden bench nestled beneath it. Many happy hours had been spent under the shade of that tree with her endless books. She drew a finger over flaking paint and splitting wood.

Ophelia meandered over to the kitchen garden and sighed. Tall weeds competed with beans and lettuce that had gone to seed. Evidence of hungry rabbits was everywhere. The vegetable plot had eagerly surrendered to nature in the few weeks since their mother's death. Her eyes scanned the shaggy lawn that also screamed for attention.

Beyond the willow and the sloping lawn, a carpet of familiar wildflowers edged the copse of trees that followed the stream. Leaving the vegetables, she wandered over to pluck some. "These will brighten up the kitchen," she said to herself.

Both sisters finally drifted back to the front door. Imogen removed the key from her handbag. "Ready?"

Ophelia nodded, clasping the violin case to her chest.

The stale air inside the cottage gasped as it leaked out, as if the ghost of their mother had been waiting to hand over the house. Though Imogen shivered, she was soon enveloped in warm, cherished memories as her gaze swung to the tightly winding staircase, scene of many sledging adventures, then down the narrow, stone-flagged hall to the promise of the cozy kitchen.

Ophelia pushed open the living room door to reveal the charming, exposed, low beams overhead and the wide, stone fireplace still adorned with a jumble of portraits and mementos of the past. Imogen reverently handled a sepia photograph of her mother and father and Ophelia felt the irrational expectation that her mother might come through the door at any moment to invite them to eat.

"I think we can splurge on new furniture, don't you?" remarked Imogen. Large scratch marks made by a cat, long since dead, marred the fabric of the armchairs that huddled close to the fireplace. "Do you want a pet?"

"Heavens, no, ducky!" replied Ophelia. "We'll have enough trouble just taking care of ourselves."

The old, grand piano crowded the front window. The lid had been left open as if their mother had merely gone to answer the door. Ophelia placed her violin on the floor beside it and ran her fingers over the keys.

Imogen dragged her hand along the dulled wood, leaving a trail. "I suppose this will need to be tuned." She sighed as the vapors of memories of piano lessons kissed the edges of her mind.

Returning to the hall, the sisters approached the beating heart of the cottage. In the middle of the irregular stone floor sat the antique farmhouse table, under a rainbow of copper pots and pans. The soft pine shone bright, bathed in a puddle of sunlight. Imogen touched the scratches and bumps developed over a lifetime.

On the far side sat the huge fireplace that had originally been the only means of cooking. "Shall we hire a cook?" Imogen asked. "I'm rather tired of preparing food myself."

"If you don't mind me experimenting, I think I can handle it," replied Ophelia, reaching under the sink for a vase.

Dried lavender hung from dark beams infusing the room with its relaxing scent as the drip of the tap on the farmhouse sink beat a steady tattoo.

After filling the vase with the fresh wildflowers, they mounted the crooked, meandering staircase. Here, Badger's Hollow revealed some of its secrets in hidden nooks and crannies. Imogen let her fingers trail along the deep sill of the little window halfway up, where she had read as a girl, wrapped in a quilt, during the winter months. She checked for the acorn doll in the small alcove on the landing. It smiled back at her.

"Do you remember picking out this floral wallpaper," sighed Ophelia as Imogen joined her in the first bedroom.

"We couldn't agree," replied Imogen. "You told me I could choose the pattern the next time we redecorated but we never did."

"Did you hate it?"

"At first. But not really." Imogen ran her eye over the antique pattern. "I grew to like it. Love it, even. It became part of the house. Part of us."

Two single beds with ragged counterpanes sat on either side of the dormer, whispering stories from the past. Artwork from their youth still hung on the walls. Two china dolls sat expressionless on the bedraggled, pine dresser.

"Do you want this room?" asked Ophelia. "I'm not bothered which one is mine. But if you'd prefer the view of the garden, you should take Mother's room."

"If you don't mind, I think I will," replied Imogen. "I find it comforting to hear the trees and the stream from the bedroom window."

"That's settled then."

They ambled into the back bedroom that still held the faint scent of their mother's favorite violet toilet water. A rush of emotions hit them both and they locked misty eyes.

"Mother lived a long and interesting life," said Imogen grabbing her sister's hand. "Remaining fiercely independent to the very end. Just as she wanted."

"True," replied Ophelia, brushing a tear from her lashes. "I don't know why I'm getting so sentimental. It's not like me."

"It's the odors more than anything. They transport one right back in time."

A large double bed with four posts reaching out to touch the low ceiling, was covered in a pastel pink bedspread. As Imogen rounded the bed, she gasped at the sight of her mother's slippers sitting neatly by the side, waiting for feet that would never return.

A lady's upholstered chair nudged the low window overlooking the garden. A basket of unfinished knitting lay at its feet.

Their mother was everywhere.

The wooden floor creaked under the thin Persian rug that had seen better days.

"If you don't mind, I *will* take this room," said Imogen, "but I'm definitely going to replace the carpet and bedding.

Maybe even give it a lick of paint. Perhaps Fergus can help me."

"Terrific idea!" agreed Ophelia. "Now, I think it's time for a cup of tea."

As they neared the bottom of the stairs, a sharp knock surprised them.

Upon opening the door, they beheld a woman dressed in every color of the spectrum. She pushed dark framed glasses up her button nose and held out a wicker basket filled with bread and tea cakes. Under her left arm was a book.

"Connie!" cried Imogen. "Come in."

Constance Featherstone leaned in to hug both the sisters. "I was so excited to hear you were moving back."

"Have you retired yet?" Imogen asked.

Connie's wrinkled face creased even more. "Retire? No! What would I do all day? I've decided I will die in the library."

"That should be interesting for children's story hour," chuckled Ophelia.

"You know what I mean," she responded, holding out the book to Imogen. "Do you still like mysteries?"

"Do I ever! Thank you."

"That is a particularly good one. There's a waiting list but when I heard you were coming back home, I snatched it." Her gray eyes twinkled. "Your mother would have loved it!"

"Without a doubt," said Ophelia, hunting in the larder for some tea while Imogen filled the kettle at the ceramic sink.

Imogen wandered over to the stove. "Blasted buttons!" she cried. "I forgot this old thing needs coal." She looked in the half-empty coal scuttle next to the oven. "It will take a while to get warm." She addressed Connie. "Do you have somewhere to be?"

"No! I cleared my calendar to come and catch up. Celina can hold the fort for the rest of the day."

"Celina?" queried Imogen.

"Mildred Chumley's grandniece. She's very organized. Keeps me on my toes. She's fluent in Dewey Decimal!" The trill laugh that Imogen remembered so well, filled the kitchen as she stoked the oven and lit the kindling with a match from a box that was laying on the top.

"Found it!" said Ophelia brandishing a small tin in triumph. "It was behind the bread bin." She pulled off the lid. "Bloomin' biscuits! It's empty!"

Connie stood. "I think your mother kept some Indian tea for the colonel." After a moment of searching, she revealed a red canister. "Here it is. Darjeeling."

Gathered around the table waiting for the water to heat, they caught up on each other's lives.

"By the way," said Connie. "The village fête is next weekend. It's going to be one to remember. We've even invited a couple of vendors from outside the village to really shake things up."

Saffron Weald had hosted a village fête since the Middle Ages. Some years were more memorable than others but one thing remained the same—it brought the villagers together and provided funds for a new church roof or the orphan's Christmas fund.

"You will come, won't you?"

"We wouldn't miss it for the world," Ophelia assured her.

# Chapter 2

After a superb night's slumber and a quick breakfast of the Indian tea, and bread from Connie's gift, Ophelia and Imogen decided it was high time to go shopping for more edibles.

"Mother used to have those huge wicker baskets," came Imogen's mumbled voice from deep within the cupboard in the tiled mud room. "Ah, here they are!" Her silver hair static from fumbling around among the old coats, Ophelia covered a grin.

"What?" demanded Imogen.

In response, Ophelia merely pointed, blue eyes twinkling.

Imogen stepped to the side to look in the mirror. "Crikey! I look like I've been through a hedge backwards!" She licked her slender fingers and smoothed down her wayward hair.

Though the twins had diametrically opposed personalities, in this, their twilight years, they both wore their white hair tucked into a low bun. However, their taste in clothing was quite different. Ophelia wore a one-of-a-kind, floral dress paired with a handmade, pink cardigan whereas Imogen was dressed in a sturdy, pleated skirt and a white, high-necked blouse.

Grabbing one of the baskets, Imogen shot her arm through the handle, while handing her sister the other, and shooed her out the door. It had rained overnight, festooning the leaves with liquid diamonds and showering the trees with a sparkling veil.

Saffron Weald was considered a hidden jewel in the British crown. Buried deep in the Hampshire countryside, on the way to nowhere, it was rare for people to happen upon it by chance. The center of the village was the high street, a narrow road flanked by Elizabethan wattle and daub buildings. Due to the primitive building methods of the sixteenth century, though all the high-gabled structures were similar, they each possessed a unique character. The upstairs peaks pushed out further than the ground floor walls, like a row of nosy matriarchs vying for position. Around the same time, a church was built as a gathering place for the inhabitants and a place to bury their dead. A couple of hundred years later, a church hall was erected in its grounds.

As the village grew, a crescent of tiny laborers' cottages was built to the east of the high street with a public house just beyond. At some point, the villagers dammed a small tributary of the River Weald to create a pond and established a green space beside it to host markets. Beyond the center, larger cottages with land were constructed, and further out still were the farms.

The original village dated from the reign of Elizabeth I and the historical society and the village council worked hard to maintain its cherished roots. One might say they had all the delicacy of an iron fist.

As the sisters entered the picturesque high street, the black and white shops winked in the morning sun.

"Do you remember when Morris Bunco from Hawthorne wanted to expand his factory-made shoe store and purchase two shops here and knock them into one?" asked Imogen.

"How could I forget?" replied Ophelia. "Mother made signs and took us to protest."

"She was a great one for preserving history."

"Makes it rather difficult for Saffron Weald to enter the twentieth century, though. Do you remember all the hours the village council spent trying to decide if they were going to permit electricity to come? Thank heavens they did!"

"Second only to the dilemma of running water and sewage lines," chuckled Imogen. "I don't think I would have agreed to come back if the cottage didn't have those things."

"Me neither," agreed Ophelia stopping outside one of the shops. "Here we are, *Tumblethorn's*." She pushed open the arched door causing the bell above it to ring.

"Ladies, ladies! Welcome home!" Reginald Tumblethorn, owner of the grocery shop, was a lively, round man in his late forties who lived with his ailing, widowed mother. He had been born after the twins left home, but they knew him from their frequent visits to their mother. He was the third Tumblethorn to run the establishment. Before that, it had been a lady's hat store with the equally unimaginative name of *Millie's.*

"How's the cottage?" he asked, straightening his colorful cravat.

"A bit shabby, if you must know," said Ophelia. "Mother liked things the way they were."

"Yes. A spirited little thing, wasn't she? She worked in her garden every fair day and always had time for a chat. I miss that. And her passing was so sudden. No lingering illness, just here one day and gone the next. But I'm sure that's a blessing when you are ninety-five."

"Except it meant we didn't get to say goodbye," Imogen pointed out.

"True," he said, using a peacock blue feather duster on the glass counter. "But you were faithful visitors. No regrets there." He straightened some lozenge tins that sat by the cash register. "Are you going to redecorate, then?"

"Once we're settled," said Ophelia.

"I can't tell you how thrilled mother and I are to have you both. Strangers would have been difficult on top of the loss of your mother."

Pretty much anyone whose name had not been recorded in the Doomsday book was considered a stranger in Saffron Weald.

"What can I do for you today?" he asked, pulling at his yellow and green plaid waistcoat as he shone a winsome smile upon them.

"The cupboard is bare at Badger's Hollow, so we're on the hunt for a few essentials," Ophelia explained.

Reginald came around the counter revealing scarlet and blue striped trousers. Neither twin batted an eye. "Well, you know how everything is organized. Help yourselves and just give me a hoot when you're ready. I'll be in the back with Mother."

"Do you have any specials today?" asked Imogen before he disappeared behind a beaded curtain. Specials were Reggie's peculiarity.

"Strawberries from Downlow Farm. Half off. Best ones in the county but on the turn." The scream of a kettle interrupted him and he disappeared with a wave.

The store was arranged in aisles that were shoulder high and all the items were arranged alphabetically; apples at the front of aisle one, biscuits next, followed by cucumbers and so forth. It was really quite a helpful system once you got used to it.

"Imogen!" cried Ophelia in a tight whisper. "Quick! Come here!"

Reginald could not help himself if offered a bargain which led to some pretty odd items finding their way onto his shelves. It was one of the reasons they made a point of frequenting the shop on their visits. Their mother would report on this month's odd item and they would all take a field trip. They had seen rubber tights, which he finally had to give away, lemon and anchovy crackers which had tasted as bad as they sound, and frightful red wigs that made anyone who tried one on resemble a clown.

Imogen approached with an expression of happy expectation. "What is it today?"

Ophelia held up a hot water bottle cover, rippling with multicolored sequins. "They would catch in your socks."

"Among other problems I see," replied Imogen. "What was he thinking?"

"You know he can't resist anything shiny. He probably got the whole lot for a pound. Two things he can't say no to."

"I can't see anyone buying one, can you?"

"Perhaps as a white elephant gift…" Ophelia said with a wicked grin.

Imogen held a dozen local eggs, a pot of raspberry jam and a tin of tea and coffee in her basket.

"Let's add flour and sugar and I can make scones for tea," suggested Ophelia.

Returning to the counter, Imogen yelled, "Yoohoo! Reginald!"

Ophelia's eyes were twinkling with mischief.

He slid through the beaded screen, wiping the corners of his mouth with a red serviette and pulling another from his shirt collar.

"Just enjoying our elevenses," he explained. "Find everything alright?"

"Tell me about the hot water bottle covers," said Ophelia with a straight face. Imogen had to look the other way.

"My cousin got them off a chap in Fulham for a song." He pressed the tips of his fingers together. "He knows me so well." His brows tried to escape his forehead. "Shall I keep one back for you?"

Ophelia coughed. "Uh, I'm not really thinking of hot water bottles in July but if you have any left when the weather cools down…" She let the sentence hang, not committing.

"Of course, we can't all be as forward thinking as I." He stuck his thumbs under his braces. "Now, let's ring you up, shall we?" He grabbed the tea. "This was the last thing your mother bought from me the day before she died. I do miss her."

As they stepped back into the high street, Imogen hit her sister on the arm. "You shouldn't tease him like that."

"Just a bit of harmless fun," responded Ophelia. "Besides, he's an innocent and completely unaware of the joshing. Now, let's visit the butcher and get some sausages, bacon and a nice lamb chop for dinner."

Harold Cleaver, the butcher, was in his mid-sixties, just a few months older than the twins. His older brother, Jeffrey Cleaver, had been Ophelia's first love. They had caused quite a stir at the time.

The butcher's shop was the trademark white stucco with jet black timbers, but thirty years ago the village council had hotly debated allowing the shop to replace the Elizabethan windows with a single pane of glass. The argument was that he needed to be able to display his wares in such a way as to entice shoppers in, which was impossible with the original windows. In a three to four vote that threatened to tear the village apart, the butcher had won. As a consequence, fresh, creamy tripe hung from hooks, red and white, thick sliced bacon beckoned from trays, and strings of sausages made Imogen's mouth water.

As they entered, a hand painted sign behind the counter proclaimed, "Cleavers. Where quality *'meats'* affordability!"

"Miss Harrington!" sang Harold, touching a hand to his straw boater with the black band. "It's been saus*ages* since I've seen you. And Mrs. Pettigrew, *poultry* in motion as usual."

"Harold," said Ophelia grimly. She hated puns. Harold chose not to notice.

"A pound of sausages, same of bacon, and two lamb chops, please," said Imogen.

"Coming right up! Settled in, have you?"

"Not really. We have plans," said Ophelia checking out the minced meat and liver.

"Plans, is it? And what might those be?" Laying wax paper on his scales he expertly placed a string of fresh sausages in the tray and whistled. "Spot on!" Wrapping them in the paper he sealed it with a piece of string and looked at them expectantly.

"New paint, change the wallpaper. Update the furniture," replied Ophelia.

He opened the case to grab two chops. "Big changes then. My grandson Pete does decorating. I'll send him round to have a look, shall I?"

"How kind," said Imogen.

"Will you be needing a gardener? I've another grandson does that." He pulled the tray of bacon from the window and peeled slices off to place on the scales.

"We intend to try and keep up with that ourselves," explained Imogen. "But in the few weeks since mother's death it has become a little overgrown. We might hire someone to tidy it up for us to begin with."

"Malcolm. He'd be perfect. I was so sad to hear of old Mrs. Harrington's passing," he said, wrapping the bacon and handing it over the counter. "She was a regular with my grandfather and father and now me, for over seventy years. Never missed a week. I enjoyed our talks—she wasn't one to *mince* words!" He chuckled at his own joke.

"One thing our mother liked was predictability," said Ophelia. "She was an interesting dichotomy really. She wasn't scared of a new challenge and heaven knows she was a free spirit at times, but she liked her daily world to be ordered and routine."

"That she did. She kept me up to date on the pair of you, too. Right proud of you she was." He eyed Ophelia. "I hope we can enjoy some musical recitals now that you'll be living here."

"I hadn't really thought about it, but I might be persuaded," she replied.

"Well, that would be a treat for sure," he responded. "That will be three shillings, please."

Imogen rummaged around in her purse and placed the three coins into his cold, beefy hand.

"You coming to the village fête?" he asked as they turned to leave. "It's going to be a corker. I was on the planning committee this year along with Reginald, Pierre, Connie, Mildred and the colonel."

"We wouldn't miss it," said Ophelia for the second time in as many days.

# Chapter 3

"I heard you were back!" said a short, plump woman wearing a broad brimmed hat with a dead bird balancing on the brim that obscured her face. She slid her shopping bags up her chubby arm and reached out her hand while pushing up the brim of the absurd hat.

"Mildred!" replied Imogen. "We couldn't see who it was."

Mildred Chumley was a decade younger than the twins and had grown up on one of the outlying farms. She had never married, though at one point it had looked close with the headmaster of the school. He had suddenly transferred to a new school, breaking her heart, and the twins had always wondered if his departure had been brought on by her constant chatter. Mildred was now the head carillonneur, president of the Women's Institute and according to Reggie, on the fête committee. She was also the local gossipmonger.

After shaking hands with them both, Mildred placed her bags on the ground and settled in for a good old natter. Ophelia smothered a sigh.

"Word is you're going to live at Badger's Hollow. So sad that your mother died but then she had a good run. I'm so sorry about your husband Imogen, but you won't get lonely living with your sister now, will you? I said to Burt Appleford, it's no good to be lonely after you become a widow. It's more than conventional wisdom, it's common sense. I thought you might go and live with your daughter but then, when the will requested you live together, well, that changed everything didn't it?" Not one breath had been taken during the whole soliloquy.

Ophelia sent a visual cry of help to her sister.

"Perfectly put," responded Imogen. "Now, if you will excuse us, we have more errands to run. I'm sure we'll see you around."

"Of course, of course." Mildred bent to pick up one of her bags. "By the way, we lost one of our ringers. I hope one of you will consider replacing him since you'll be living here now. It's a great way to become ensconced in the community." A hint of desperation leaked from her beady eyes.

"We've only been here five minutes," declared Ophelia. Imogen stepped on her toe. "But as soon as we're settled, we'll think about it."

"Well, don't take too long," Mildred announced to their backs. "We have a couple of weddings coming up and it won't sound the same with one missing."

Ophelia waved a hand in the air as they pushed their way into the sweet shop, *The Jolly Lolly*.

"Phew!" she declared. "I thought we were never going to get away."

A stick thin woman with a long nose and friendly eyes leaned over the counter to look out the window. "Mildred." She nodded sagely. "She can be a bit much before lunch. Can I get you anything or did you just bolt in here as a means of escape?"

Imogen smiled. "You're very perceptive. I don't think we've met?"

The woman smiled back. "Arabella Fudgeford. We bought the place from Cedric Lollington after his stroke. His son put him in a nice nursing home near his house in Parkford. I've always loved Saffron Weald. I grew up in Sudbridge and my mother used to bring us to visit an old cousin who lived on her own here. It was always a treat to come to the sweet shop. As soon as I saw it was for sale, I talked to my husband Fred about buying it. Been here six months now."

"I'm Imogen Pettigrew and this is my twin sister, Ophelia Harrington."

"Nice to meet you, though I should tell you you're the talk of the town—or village I should say."

"I don't doubt it," chuckled Ophelia. "And you're spot on about our escape but now that I'm in here, I've a hankering for some black licorice. I'll take a quarter of a pound, please."

Arabella was so tall, she didn't need a ladder to reach the large, clear sweet canisters on the second shelf. "How do you feel about coming back? I'm sure it's quite different from how it was in the 1860s." She unscrewed the large, black lid and tipped the rich licorice pieces onto the scales.

"Not as different as you might imagine," said Ophelia with a wry grin. "Saffron Weald does not embrace change."

"That much I've learned," replied Arabella. "When we tried to buy the place there was quite a lot of opposition. But now that we're established, I think it's one of the things I like about the place."

She tipped the licorice into a small, white bag, swung it around three times and handed the neatly closed package to Ophelia.

"It's a safe place for my children, Samantha and Cedric. They love it here."

"Bella!" A man with a high voice was calling for her.

"Out front, Fred."

An extremely short man, as wide as he was tall, entered the shop front from the back.

"Oh, hello!" He emphasized the 'e', his eyes darting back and forth between the sisters. "And who do we have here?"

"These are the twin sisters we've heard so much about, Fred. The ones that are going to live in Mrs. Harrington's cottage. These are her daughters."

Fred Fudgeford resembled a panda bear. Ophelia had come face to face with one on a safari through China thirty years before. His large, round face was pale as paper, but dark circles smudged like bruises under each eye.

He ran a hand over his sparse, black hair before reaching over the counter to shake hands. "Well, isn't this an honor? I simply ad*o*red your mother!" Apparently, 'e's weren't the only vowel in Fred's toolbox. "I'm sure you know she had a rather sweet tooth?"

"Oh, yes!" replied Imogen. "And her teeth showed it. She had to be fitted for porcelain ones in her early fifties. She hated how they tasted and felt but was too proud to go out in public without them."

"It didn't seem to stop her from indulging." Fred beamed so hard his eyes disappeared.

"Indeed," replied Imogen. "My children loved to visit as she always had sweets out in little glass dishes."

"Always," agreed Ophelia.

"My parents do the same thing," Arabella piped in. "Anything for you, Mrs. Pettigrew?"

"Oh, please call me Imogen." She ran her eyes over the colorful, sugary treats. "I'll have some rhubarb and custards."

"A quarter pound, do you?"

"Yes, please."

These were on the lower shelf and Fred Fudgeford retrieved the glass cannister and handed it to his wife.

"Well, *we* think it is w*o*nderful that the cottage is staying in the family." Fred's pale face shone with goodwill. "Welcome home."

"Thank you," said Imogen reaching for the bag and handing some change over the counter.

"We hope you will keep your mother's sweetie tradition alive," he said, tapping the tips of his fingers together.

"I think you can be sure of that," declared Ophelia.

Once on the pavement, Ophelia looked up the street. "My bag is getting rather heavy. What else, do you think?"

"I know Connie brought us bread yesterday, but it's so much better fresh. Do you mind if we get a cob loaf?"

"Bread isn't too heavy," Ophelia assured her. "But let's go home after that."

Laden with supplies, they entered the *Golden Crust* bakery. The heavenly scent of fresh bread was baked into every brick. Crusty loaves smiled at them from each shelf like old friends.

Ophelia rang the bell that sat on the counter.

Within seconds a man who evidently sampled his wares freely, covered from head to foot in white flour, appeared.

"If it isn't the Harrington girls! It's so good to see you." His wrinkles made crevices in the flour.

Archie Puddingfield was a few years younger than the twins. In his youth he had been incredibly attractive and was a marvel on the violin. Almost as good as Ophelia. They had all played together in the local amateur orchestra.

"Alice!" he bellowed. "Look who's here!"

His wife came through, pushing clouds of flour away with delicate hands. She was still a beauty at sixty. Archie had met her in Brighton when the orchestra went on tour in the 1870s. Alice had been in the front row, and Archie was first violin after Ophelia left for London. Their eyes had met and it was love at first sight. The kind of romantic love story you read about in novels.

"Imogen! Ophelia! Welcome home!" Alice embraced both women in a puff of floury rosewater.

Though she was from a modern seaside town, Alice had adapted well to small village life. With one exception. Archie's family had run the bakery since the time of Charles I, and resided in the apartment above, but Alice refused to live there. So, they had bought a neat little cottage on the east side of the village.

"Saffron Weald needs shaking up, and you are just the two to do it!" Alice declared.

"What can I get you?" asked Archie rubbing his hands on his apron.

"We'll take one cob, please," replied Imogen. "There's nothing quite like it to make one feel at home."

"Can't disagree with that," replied Archie, wrapping the loaf in white paper and handing it to Imogen. "And it's on the house. A welcome back gift, if you will."

"That's very kind of you," Imogen responded.

"Let's make plans to get together soon." added Alice.

As the sisters headed for the door they were almost bowled over by a thin, attractive man in a neat suit, a monocle clamped to his eye.

# Chapter 4

"Ladies! Ladies! A thousand apologies." The monocle now swung from its chain as he leaned in to give them each the French greeting.

"Pierre! Oh, it's you. I almost dropped my bread," declared Imogen, bracing herself on the door frame as he kissed her cheeks.

"Hello, Pierre."

Imogen snapped her head toward her sister. There was something in her tone. Something secret. Something understood. And his kisses on Ophelia's cheeks were slower, more deliberate.

"Ophelia. So, it *is* true. You 'ave come back to sleepy Saffron Weald. For good." His smile was like the sunrise, slow at first but eventually filling his whole face with light.

"It rather seems that way," said Ophelia, her eye trained on Pierre's sculpted face.

Imogen suddenly felt like an outsider, one who isn't privy to an inside joke.

"I am simply enchanted that our village will now 'ost such refined and educated ladies." Even after twenty years in Saffron Weald, he had not quite lost the accent that women found so alluring.

Imogen felt herself succumbing to its charm and twittered, "Pierre, you really *are* the limit."

"How's business? We might pop in later," added Ophelia. "We've decided to upgrade Mother's furniture. We want something comfortable, above all. And sturdy."

Pierre crossed his arms, one hand stroking his clipped, snow-white beard. "You're in luck! I'm taking possession of some quality goods from an estate sale in Kent on Friday. Can you wait till I 'ave inventoried it all?" He looked from one sister to the other, a question in his sparkling brown eyes.

"Of course. We have plenty of other things to get started on, like the garden," responded Ophelia.

"Good." He ran a finger down the lapel of his tailored tweed suit. "I shall expect you Monday." Tipping his hat, he popped the single glass that was really just for show, into his breast pocket. "After the fête."

"Will you be participating?" Ophelia asked, adjusting her gloves.

"Certainly. I always 'ave my curiosities stand and besides, I am on the organizing committee this year."

"We'll see you there, then. Come on, Imogen."

Pierre Ancien stepped aside to let them pass and Imogen caught a fleeting glimpse of teenage Ophelia.

"Is there something I should know?" asked Imogen as they started for home, lugging their heavy baskets.

"Whatever are you talking about?" asked Ophelia looking straight ahead.

"The air was rather charged back there."

Tucking in her chin and shaking her head, Ophelia's mouth shrugged. "I don't know what you mean, ducky. Pierre has always flirted with any woman he meets. It's how he's been so successful as a foreigner in an English village."

It is said that twins have a special sense that connects them. Identical twins, even more so, and Imogen felt it now. But she also knew her sister well enough to know when a subject was closed. Imogen would acquiesce for the moment, but she had no intention of letting the matter drop for good.

"My arms ache. Let's sit for a bit," she suggested as the village green with its picturesque pond came into view. She was feeling the weight of her burden in her arthritic shoulders.

"If you insist," agreed Ophelia. "Are you alright, ducky?"

"Fine, I just have weak shoulders. We might have to shop more often for smaller quantities or get wheels on these things."

"It is rather cumbersome," agreed Ophelia. "We should have asked if any of the shops have a delivery service." She sat on the bench her father had provided, hardly noticing the plaque announcing the fact, and patted the seat next to her. Imogen placed the grocery basket at her feet.

As a pretty mother swan and her signets swam seamlessly by, Imogen lamented, "I should have brought some of yesterday's bread."

"It's not like we planned this and do you really want to add another thing to our bags?"

"Well, when you put it like that." Imogen kept her eyes on the graceful swans.

"And she looks perfectly content as she is," continued Ophelia.

The bench faced the pond whose backdrop was the Medieval Gothic church, its coursed limestone bell tower soaring into the clouds.

"That reminds me, what do you think about joining the ringers?" asked Ophelia.

"Not with this arthritis," responded Imogen. "It's from the fall."

"From Buttercup," Ophelia nodded. "I remember it well. Father told you to get right back on or you'd have a life-long fear."

"Just as well he did, or I would never have won all those medals."

"What did you do with those?" asked Ophelia, placing her arm along the back of the bench.

"Penny wanted them." Her brows rounded. "Can't see why."

"You were a county champion," blustered Ophelia. "Of course, she's proud."

Imogen shrugged. "So, what about you?"

Ophelia frowned.

"The ringers?" Imogen reminded her.

"Oh. I'd say it rather depends on who the others are."

"Mrs. Pettigrew! Miss Harrington!" The sisters twisted in their seat at the familiar sound of the affable vicar. "It's like I'm seeing double!"

"Reverend Cresswell!" beamed Imogen. "What a pleasant surprise!"

The old vicar, Reverend Bertrand Fossilworth, had expired on his ninety-ninth birthday some years before. Even their mother, who was a faithful church attendee, had become frustrated at his old ways and the whole village had embraced the new, younger vicar, his wife and three children, with open arms.

To describe his features as bland would have been generous. It was as though he had been molded out of pale clay and the sculptor had tired of the project before finishing. The only interesting features were his eyes, not that their hazel coloring was noteworthy, but that they sparkled with the fire of authentic, devoted charity.

"Sit! Sit!" demanded Ophelia.

The vicar glanced at his watch. "I daresay I can spare five minutes."

He wore a dark suit with his dog collar and Imogen wondered if he was sweating in the increasing heat of the July day.

"I was planning to pay you ladies a visit soon. When would be a good time?"

"Oh, I'm sure you're far too busy to bother with us," replied Imogen.

The vicar looked offended. "It is a parochial duty I dare not shirk. And nothing would give me more pleasure. Do you need any help with moving in your things?"

"We're only bringing our clothes and a few odds and ends. Most of it is being delivered tomorrow," explained

Ophelia. "We'll eventually replace the furniture, but I'm sure they offer a delivery option."

"Then, if you're sure, I shall pay you a visit around teatime tomorrow. It's not often I receive an addition to my flock."

Truer words had never been spoken. Saffron Weald was allergic to change of any kind. Other than the vicar and his family, and the sweet shop owners, the last move-ins had been the florist's family and they had moved in over fifteen years ago.

"Well, we're not really new additions," Ophelia pointed out. "This was where we were born and raised."

The vicar's shoulders jumped up and down and a sputtering laugh like a cold engine trying to start, spilled from his mouth. "Oh, to be sure, to be sure!" He slapped his thigh. "But since you are new to me, I shall consider you new parishioners. Is that tickety-boo?"

"You're welcome any time, vicar," responded Imogen. "I know Mother was extremely fond of you."

"I spent many hours in your mother's lovely parlor." He shifted on the bench. "I don't suppose either of you knows how to make her delicious coffee cake?" His whole face repositioned into a question mark.

"That would be Ophelia's department," replied Imogen. "I'm strictly meat and two veg."

"For you vicar, I will hunt down her recipe book," added Ophelia. "Shall we say four?"

"Splendid! I can tell you all about the fête. It's going to be an event for the history books!"

# Chapter 5

Creeping over the horizon at four forty-seven, the sun began its daily climb. Kissing the crepey eyelids of the twin sisters with its warmth as they basked in dreams spawned by the mists of childhood memories, its light woke them.

Eager to begin tidying the garden, the sisters rose in tandem at five o'clock, gliding through the wispy dew that hung over the long grass, and clung to their skirts.

"I'll take the kitchen garden," declared Ophelia. "See if I can find any kind of harvest among the weeds."

"I'll see to the front flower beds," replied Imogen.

Saffron Weald was just waking up, bathed in a hazy summer light. Birds were already busy hunting worms for hungry chicks. Bees emerging from hidden hives to gather pollen, buzzed under Imogen's nose as she attacked the roses with shears and pulled weeds that strangled the bushes.

By seven o'clock, with two hours of work under their belts, they both collapsed onto the kitchen chairs hardly able to heat water for tea. A small cache of green beans and peas was all the bounty Ophelia had managed to harvest.

"Remember how Mr. Cleaver suggested one of his grandsons?" asked Imogen, "That's looking like a better idea all the time. We're not thirty anymore, lovey."

"I agree. This is far more work than I anticipated. I'm all for pottering about but this heavy lifting is a little more than I wish to handle."

"Oh, I'm so glad. I thought you were going to tell me I was being wimpy!" Imogen leaned her head on the cool table. "I might need to take a nap soon."

Ophelia's shoulders shook as she silently laughed and it took her a minute to be able to speak. "Look at us! A pair of broken-down old ladies. When did that happen?"

"It creeps up on you. Suddenly there's a strange old biddy staring back at you from the mirror. I still *feel* twenty most days. Do you remember how we used to impatiently criticize the elderly for their sluggishness? And here we are now, old ourselves. The objects of today's young people's judgement."

"At least we don't shuffle yet. Mother tried so hard not to shuffle but, in the end, she had no control over it." Ophelia pulled yesterday's bread toward her and cut two healthy pieces.

"Do you remember when Broomfield's in Westerbridge had just got a shipment of the latest spring bonnets in 1880 and Mrs. Pinkerton happened to be ahead of us in line? I had to stop myself stamping my feet in despair and sighing loudly as she counted out the pennies for her purchase."

"And now it's us causing the young to get impatient," lamented Ophelia.

"I sense it with my own grandchildren," agreed Imogen, pulling the butter and bread toward her. "Speed is sacrosanct to the young. We were going to a local horse show and Amelia's latest young man was going to be there. Seeing the weather was on the turn, I declared that I was going to get a cardigan. Amelia actually rolled her eyes."

"Would you trade youth for the wisdom you've gained, though?" asked Ophelia, rising to pour hot water onto the leaves in the old tea pot with the hairline crack.

Imogen huffed. "No. I endorse the old maxim; *youth is wasted on the young*."

"Now, if I could go back with all—"

A knock on the door interrupted Ophelia's soapbox speech.

"Who on earth?" It was still only half past seven in the morning.

"I'll go," said Imogen, pushing herself up by using the tabletop as leverage.

She wandered down the uneven stone of the hall, careful not to shuffle, and opened the door. Upon the doorstep was a very good looking, tall and well-built young man, with shaggy hair and a threadbare shirt. "Malcom Cleaver. My grandpa sent me. Said you might be needing some help with your garden."

Imogen clapped her hands together. "Oh, bless you, lovey! How serendipitous! We've spent the last two hours working our fingers to the bone and you can hardly tell. We were just this moment deciding that we needed to hire someone. Come in, come in!" She stood back and let him enter before showing him into the kitchen.

"Just as I remember," he said, tipping his head in greeting.

"You've been here before?" asked Ophelia.

"Your mum used to give me piano lessons years ago. She would treat me to tea and biscuits after. Right here in this kitchen while she sang opera."

Imogen shook her head at the memory. "Opera. How she loved it. You do too, don't you Ophelia?"

"I am a fully paid member of the London Opera Society," she replied, proudly. "Just wait till I find her gramophone records. Opera is best enjoyed at full volume. Don't you agree, ducky?" she asked the young gardener.

His rugged chin dropped, pulling his whole face down. "Never took to it, myself."

"Oh, I'm with you, Malcolm. It *is* an acquired taste," Imogen agreed. "Let's pour you some tea before you start."

For the next fifteen minutes the sisters laid out their plans for the garden and Malcolm interrupted with very sensible questions until they had beaten out a plan and suitable pecuniary remuneration.

As he headed outside, Imogen declared that she was going upstairs for a cat nap.

"Well, all that talk about opera has got me itching," opined Ophelia. "I'm going to hunt for mother's records.

I'll keep it low until you arise." She winked and trilled, "Ah, ha,ha,ha,a-a-a-a!" the famous aria from the Magic Flute, something she had done for as long as Imogen could remember. Imogen sang back to her the next line, while Ophelia responded with the third.

"We're going to have such fun together, ducky," said Ophelia with a glimmer in her eye. "Now, off you go to get some beauty sleep."

By lunch time, Malcolm had mowed the lawn and begun to hack back the trees and bushes that had overgrown. He was to come every day until the garden was under control then twice a week after that.

Imogen awoke, invigorated by her nap, and Ophelia had found and dusted off a stack of her mother's operatic gramophone records instead of looking for the recipe book.

"I'll have *my* symphonic and jazz records sent from my flat as soon as I can." Ophelia had opted to keep her flat in Chelsea as it was convenient if they traveled to town for a play or the symphony.

Imogen's mouth pulled down. "Jazz?"

"Oh, yes! There are some fabulous bands now. I'll have to try to convert you."

A sharp knock drew their attention. They locked eyes and shrugged.

"Must be the vicar. I'll go this time," said Ophelia. Imogen wandered after her.

A hale and hearty, upright man whom they immediately recognized, stood on the doorstep before them.

"Colonel Winstanley!"

"Thought I'd pop by to make an official welcome back to the village, and all that." He spoke in the clipped staccato of his trade.

Colonel Winstanley had grown up in the village, left to seek his fortune in his majesty's armed forces, risen to the rank of colonel, and retired back to Saffron Weald after his wife died. He was more than a decade older than the twins but had always been a force to be reckoned with. He continued to wield his considerable influence among the villagers to this day as current head of the village council.

"Come in, Colonel. Can we offer you some tea?"

Having served for many years in India, they already knew he was a stickler for the Indian Darjeeling tea, which was why their mother had kept some in a separate tin, although she hated the stuff.

"Splendid." He marched in, wedging his leather gloves under his armpit and striding to the kitchen.

Pulling out one of the scruffy chairs he asked, "How are you both settling in?"

"Very well, thank you," replied Ophelia.

He looked around the scruffy kitchen. "Fine woman your mother. Great loss to the village. Always busy. Began writing a history of the place before her death."

Imogen stopped burrowing into the larder. "She was? Did you know, Ophelia?"

"No. I thought we already had an amateur historian in the village. Algernon something or other."

"Wainwright. Yes. Records all the dates of events and that kind of thing. No, your mother told me hers was more about the personalities that made up the place over the centuries and how they molded the village."

"She never told us," said Imogen, holding aloft the almost empty cannister of dark, Darjeeling.

"I shall make it a point to look for her notes," declared Ophelia. "Perhaps we could finish it and get it published."

"Are you coming to the fête on Saturday?" the colonel asked. "We've pulled out all the stops this year, you know. We've some outside vendors coming. One is bringing a small Ferris wheel—"

"Ooh! How exciting," interrupted Ophelia.

"And another will be selling authentic fish and chips. It was a bit pricy but I think it will attract people from all over the county and we'll make our money back and then some." He ran a finger along his gloves. "They're a bit short handed for some of the games. Don't suppose you could help with the egg and spoon race and tug of war?"

"We'd love to," Imogen answered for both of them. She poured hot water over the black leaves, replaced the lid and slid a cozy over the top. Then, arranging some of the treats Connie had brought over, she carried them both to the table.

"I was sorry to hear about your husband, Imogen. Was it unexpected?" the colonel asked.

Wilfred Pettigrew, country accountant who specialized in estate planning, had died at his desk on a Thursday afternoon, two weeks before officially retiring.

"Horribly," she replied. "Heart attack."

"My Lilith died while out riding. Took a fall." He shrugged. "She died doing what she loved most."

"Wilfred and I had plans to travel Europe once he retired. I was quite looking forward to it, but now that he's gone…"

"We could still go, ducky. You and I," declared Ophelia, who had never let being single hold her back from traveling extensively. "Nothing stopping us. I remember visiting France when I was younger. The South is lovely."

"Perhaps," replied Imogen, straining the tea for the colonel and offering sugar and milk.

"What do you do these days, Colonel?" asked Ophelia.

"I'm adamant about exercising the body and brain. I collect butterflies and stamps and lead the local ramblers club. You should consider joining."

Ophelia frowned. "Is there an amateur dramatics club? That's more my line."

"Yes, they put on two plays a year at the village hall. They have a production coming up after the fête. Matilda Butterworth runs it, I believe."

"Is she the one who runs the tea shop?"

"That's her. Bit bossy but overall, I think she does a good job." He took a sip and winced.

"Mildred Chumley said they're looking for another bell ringer," said Ophelia. "What happened to the last one?"

"Alfred Tingey? Hit by a bus on a trip to London. It was his first and last visit to our nation's capital."

"*Hot crumpets*! That's terrible!" declared Imogen, pretending to like the strong brew.

"Yes, it was rather. His wife was present and watched it happen. Hasn't been the same since."

"I should think not!" cried Imogen.

"Mildred wants one of us to take his place," explained Ophelia. "Imogen has dodgy shoulders though."

The colonel pursed his lips. "That so."

"Do you think it's a bad idea?" Imogen asked.

"Far be it from me to speak ill of someone…"

"But…" added Ophelia.

"Let's just say Mildred is a hard taskmaster." This was criticism indeed from the colonel who still ruled his life with military precision.

Ophelia tapped the side of her nose. "Duly noted, Colonel. Thanks for the tip."

The colonel drained his cup. "Well, I must be going. Got a hundred things still to do before Saturday. Thanks for the tea."

Once the colonel left, Imogen stole outside and headed for the willow with the book Connie had brought. The cottage windows were open to make a cross breeze, and the muted strains of Wagner cloaked the garden.

Under the protective shade of the willow's branches, Imogen dived into the engaging mystery and was soon immersed. So much so, that she was unaware of the vicar's arrival until Ophelia brought him out into the garden with a full tea tray.

"Reverend Cresswell," Imogen said, shading her eyes. "How delightful."

"We haven't found mother's recipe book yet, I'm afraid, so no famous coffee cake," explained Ophelia. "Which is odd since she used to keep it on the middle shelf of the larder."

"No matter." He took a seat next to Imogen while Ophelia went on the hunt for a garden chair. As she struggled back, the vicar jumped to her aid.

"We were all surprised to hear of your mother's passing," he said between sips. "She had been to church the day before and appeared to be in fine fettle. She never lost that keen wit."

"And we appreciate the lovely service you held for her." The family had gathered in Saffron Weald for the funeral. The whole village had turned out for one of its oldest residents. But funerals choke the mind, leaving little emotional space for real conversation and though they must have seen and spoken to most of the village that day, it was a grief-filled blur.

"It was a pleasure." He took a bite of a stale biscuit. "Mrs. Harrington continued her involvement in civic matters to the very end. Her tenure on the historical preservation society was legendary and she never missed teaching Sunday School if she could help it. Might we count on you two to fill her shoes?"

"I think I can speak for both of us," began Ophelia, "when I say that we would be honored to replace mother in the Sunday School but as for the historical society—I think that position would be better suited to a different personality."

Imogen telegraphed her gratitude. The last thing she wanted to do was spend her retirement fighting with a bunch of over-zealous bureaucrats over windowpanes and paint colors.

    The vicar rubbed his hands together. "Splendid." Pulling a folded piece of paper from his pocket he handed it to Ophelia who showed it to her sister.

    "It's a calendar of monthly and special events," he explained, pointing to Saturday which was marked 'fête'.

    "Oh, yes!" Imogen assured him. "The colonel visited us earlier and recruited us to help with a couple of the games."

    "Excellent! Well, I should be going. Thanks for the tea. And if you need anything don't hesitate. You know where I live." The cold engine sputtered to life as he laughed at his little joke.

# Chapter 6

The day of the fête dawned glorious.
British weather was predictably unpredictable which led to a national talent for creating contingency plans, but the twins doubted those would be needed today. And the red sunset the night before had promised fine weather all day.
After a morning of gentle gardening, thanks to Malcolm, they both took a bath before the afternoon's entertainment.
Ophelia descended the stairs in a scarlet and cream, drop-waist creation with matching cloche hat that Imogen felt might look better on someone thirty years younger, but she kept such opinions to herself. She had chosen a light, thin cotton skirt with a lace collar blouse paired with a straw hat.
As usual the fête was taking place on the village green with the church and pond as a rustic backdrop. When the village was first established, the green was used for a thriving weekly marketplace for the sale of animals and vegetables, but today it served as a place of respite and relaxation—the perfect place for the entertainment. The curve of quaint, low cottages with thatched roofs edged the green space. And since it was the middle of summer, a riot of colorful flowers sang from their wooden window boxes.
A little removed from the dwellings sat the only village pub, the Dog and Whistle. When the inn was first created in 1543, it had been named the Hexed Cauldron because of the popularity of witch trials in the country but by the early 1700s such things had passed out of favor and the village council voted to change the name to something less polarizing. Today, Desmond Ale, the proprietor had flung open his doors with a sign listing his hearty menu at reduced prices.

An enormous, white refreshment tent sat on one side of the green, and the Ferris wheel and other carnival attractions on the other. The middle had been roped off for the various children's races.

A sudden whiff of manure gave away the location of the pony rides as Ophelia and Imogen made for the colonel who was brandishing a clipboard while in heated conversation with Mildred Chumley.

As they approached, Mildred, scarlet faced, turned on her heel and stalked away, muttering under her breath.

The colonel stared after her, jaw strained.

"Colonel," said Imogen.

His head turned but his eyes were still distant. "What? Oh, ladies. How good of you to come early. Last minute fires to put out."

"Anything serious?"

"No, nothing I can't handle. Now, here's what I would like you to do."

The sisters had retrieved a whistle and a long piece of tape from the colonel and were awaiting the official opening of the fête under the shade of the three-hundred-year-old oak.

"Do you think the Ferris wheel operator will let me on early, before the crowds arrive?" asked Ophelia.

"No harm in asking. You could suggest that you are prepared to be a guinea pig."

"Don't you want to come, ducky?"

Imogen shuddered at the thought. "No. I'm quite content to see you try it."

She watched as her sister walked gracefully toward the bearded wheel operator. A pipe hung from his slack lips and a time-worn hat protected his weathered skin from the bright, summer sunshine. He tipped his head as her sister asked her question then pushed the hat back from his forehead, looking up at his contraption. Finally, he nodded. Helping Ophelia into one of the swinging carriages he slammed the door shut and proceeded to his operating station.

As the wheel began its slow ascent, Imogen heard a youthful squeal of delight from her sister who was now at least thirty feet off the ground. She began to fling her arms around making the small carriage swing dangerously and Imogen was very glad she had declined her sister's offer. She clutched her stomach.

After three full rotations, the wheel slowed until it stopped and the man helped Ophelia from the carriage. She began to sprint toward Imogen, cheeks pink, eyes sparkling, an echo of the vibrant young woman she had once been.

"You should have tried it, Imogen. On such a day as this I could see for miles."

"I am quite content to experience it through your description, lovey," she replied, watching as the operator wiped his brow with a colorful handkerchief and took a swig of amber liquid she suspected came from the Dog and Whistle.

A young, slender woman sporting a tightly curled bob and a becoming pink dress, made her way across the green toward the colonel who was still wielding his clipboard. She was not someone Imogen recognized.

As the young woman spoke, the strain slipped from the colonel's face and he began to nod with enthusiasm, pointing toward the tea tent. The girl appeared to thank him and started to make her way over to the pavilion when she spotted the twin sisters and stopped in her tracks. After a moment of indecision, she switched direction and made for them as they sat under the shade of the tree. By this time, villagers were beginning to enter the green in anticipation of the opening.

"How do you do? My name is Lila Winterbourne. I'm covering the fête for the county newspaper." She stuck out a delicate hand. "Do you mind answering a few questions?"

"Lila. What a lovely name," said Imogen shaking the limp hand. "Of course, though I'm not sure we can tell you much."

"Let me be the judge of that." Lila pulled a pencil from her frizzy, light hair. "Are you from the village?"

Ophelia briefly explained the situation.

"Twin sisters who return to the village where they were born, in their twilight years. It's so endearing," gushed the girl. "Would make a great article."

The sisters shared a look.

"So, you didn't take part in the organization of the fête?" Lila asked.

"No. We're old friends of the colonel." Imogen pointed back to Colonel Winstanley who was talking to other villagers. "He explained they were a bit short of help and asked if we would volunteer."

"Old friends? Has the colonel always lived here?"

Ophelia could tell she was angling for some kind of romantic background story. "No. Like us, he has returned. He married while we were still in school, ducky. Much older than us."

Lila did not seem the least embarrassed by her faux pas. "When did he return?" she persisted.

"About ten years ago, give or take," replied Ophelia.

"Some never leave and others of us, return," Imogen said, helpfully. "Saffron Weald is a very nice place to live."

"I'm sure." Lila withdrew a notebook from a satchel that hung from her narrow shoulder. "I'm hoping to add a historical depth to my piece. I'm wondering if it might not be the oldest fête in the country." She flicked her head but the tight curls stayed put. "Did you attend the fête when you were young?"

"Every year," responded Ophelia. "It's the center of the village calendar. Second only to the Christmas Ball held in the village hall."

The journalist's eyes dipped down at the outer corners giving her a whimsical air. "What kind of events did you enjoy back when you were girls?"

"Much the same," replied Ophelia. "Except for the Ferris Wheel of course. Today we're running the egg and spoon race and the tug of war. Those were favorites of ours when we were children."

"There was the sack race and the family relay, too," added Imogen. "I imagine those will also take place today."

"Don't forget the bonny baby contest and the animal best of fair," added Ophelia. "We won our fair share of blue ribbons back then."

"What do you think of the new additions? Like the Ferris wheel?" Lila asked turning to look at the contraption.

Ophelia clasped her hands as if about to sing a solo for an opera and Imogen knew she was settling in for a lecture. "Although our village values its history, I believe it's important to move with the times to some extent. Keeps the event fresh and vital. That attracts new visitors. This is, after all, a charitable fundraiser."

Lila's dark blue eyes narrowed. "Yes, I'm hoping to interview the vicar. I believe the money goes to the widows and orphans fund this year." She looked around as if expecting the vicar to appear. "What year did you say you moved away from Saffron Weald?"

"In 1884 when I married," Imogen explained.

"I moved to London in 1885 just after my sister left," said Ophelia. "I lived in one room and barely survived on a small allowance from my parents. I played in amateur orchestras for no money until I got a job with the Queen's Hall Orchestra in 1913. I was one of six violinists they hired in a triumph for women musician's everywhere."

"Uh-oh," thought Imogen. "She's angling for the journalist to do a piece on her."

"Interesting." However, Lila did not bite and her tone made an oxymoron of her comment. She looked toward the tea tent once more. "What was it like being identical twins in a small village? Did you ever try to trick people?"

Ophelia glanced at Imogen with a mischievous glint. Imogen nodded approval.

"I'm no good at mathematics and Imogen was not good at French. When we were about fourteen, I took Imogen's French exam and she took my maths one. No one ever found out."

The journalist's expression evolved. Evidently, this was something she *did* find interesting. "Go on! I bet you got up to all sorts."

"Well, there was the time when William Smoot asked me to walk out with him," said Ophelia, "but I couldn't go that day. I had liked him for months and I didn't want him to ask someone else, so Imogen went in my stead."

"Oh, yes!" said Imogen, the memory coming back in fits and starts. "I had to dress and try to talk like you. It's not as easy as you'd think. I had to consider every sentence and use some of your unique expressions like '*flaming fiddles*'!"

"And he didn't suspect?" asked Lila.

"Nope," replied Ophelia. "The next time he asked, I was able to go and he didn't act like anything was amiss. We courted that whole summer."

The vicar popped his head out of the refreshment tent. "Oh, I must go," declared Lila. "I want to interview him. It's been a pleasure."

With a sort of skipping, brisk step, Lila hurried over to catch Reverend Cresswell.

"I bet it's not often the vicar is so popular," declared Ophelia.

"No. And she's not a very good journalist" declared Imogen. "She didn't even ask our names."

# Chapter 7

As did many villages, Saffron Weald possessed its own nobleman. However, the village outdated his genealogical line by at least two hundred years. In the early eighteenth century, a newly minted viscount had been in search of a swath of land upon which to build his estate. Finding a suitable site just north of the village on a gentle rise that presented panoramic views of the village in the shallow valley that led down to the river Weald, he bought the property on first sight. Legend had it that the original viscount had been so moved by the beauty of the place that he had paid three times the asking price. Ophelia doubted it very much.

The resulting, lavish Stirling Manor had reflected the neo-classical architecture of his time with many windows, surprising because of the sticky window tax. It was a strictly symmetrical, pillared structure made of local stone and light-colored brick. The dark slate roof boasted many dormers and a balustrade with a weather cupola dead center. It was not unattractive but neither was it in keeping with the Elizabethan style of the rest of Saffron Weald, and as such, had not been embraced by the villagers.

Since the original Lord Stirling had arrived in the village well after its establishment, the villagers had never felt beholden to the titled gent as their master. However, on such occasions as the opening of the annual fête, he was a useful idiot. The current Lord Stirling was forty-three, married to a horsey woman in looks and disposition and had begotten four very naughty children.

The fête attendees were gathered around the brightly draped dais as Lord Stirling blathered on about this and that before the colonel gave him a signal to get on with it, and he cut the ribbon for the official opening of the fair. The crowd whooped and hollered, then scattered like so many baby spiders, to the various stalls and activities.

Since the races were later in the afternoon, the two sisters wandered around looking at the stalls; pottery, jam, local honey and Pierre's knick-knacks.

"Imogen! Ophelia! Bonjour! You look heavenly!"

Was it in Imogen's imagination or had he laid more emphasis on Ophelia's name?

"Come and peruse my little offerings." He wore a cream, linen suit with a Panama hat and looked the epitome of an Englishman.

Imogen fingered some brass candlesticks and delicate patterned, china teacups while Ophelia and Pierre made small talk. After looking through everything twice, the smell of the fish and chip stand lured them over and they each bought a helping of chips, bathed in salt and vinegar.

Every now and again the colonel appeared, flapping about like a mother hen, the clipboard still grafted to his hand.

"If the colonel doesn't watch out, he's likely to have a stroke," commented Imogen. "It happened to our bank manager during the war. One day he was a healthy fifty-year-old and the next he was dead."

Catching sight of them, the colonel hurried over. "All ready? We want to start the egg and spoon race in five minutes. We'll make an announcement."

"We're headed back this very moment, Colonel. Why don't you go and have a cup of tea?" suggested Imogen.

"No time for that, I'm afraid. One of the tea ladies hasn't shown up, the coconut shy man was half an hour late and I can't find the journalist. Said she was going to interview me at three. I said I could give her five minutes."

"Well, don't run yourself ragged."

"Hmm." He was scanning the crowds rather than paying attention. "Must go!" he declared and strode off on his long legs.

A small crowd of children were lined up by the cordoned area waiting for the races, clutching coconuts, sweets and various toys.

"I think it best if one of us is at the start and one at the finish," said Ophelia.

"How can we hold the finish line up if we're alone?" asked Imogen.

"Grab an older child to help. I'm headed to the start." Ophelia pulled the whistle from her pocket, grabbed the box holding the spoons and boiled eggs and called to the crowd of children to follow her. She had missed her calling as a primary school teacher.

A boy of about thirteen was on the verge of following her, but Imogen managed to stop him. "I say, could you help me with the finish line?"

The boy did a double take and glanced at the disappearing form of Ophelia. "Cor, you look just like 'er!"

"Yes, we're identical twins. Now, how about helping me out? I'll make it worth your while." She flashed a thruppenny bit and the boy smiled.

"Just tell me what to do, missus."

After ten egg and spoon races for different ages, Ophelia declared the activity finished and the children scattered.

"Let's get some tea before the tug of war," Imogen suggested. "The schedule says it's not till half past four."

The refreshment tent was rather stuffy even though the doors had been tied open. The enclosed space was teaming with humanity.

"You find a table and I'll get us the tea and cakes," said Ophelia.

"Righty-ho," replied Imogen.

She glanced around the room but saw no empty tables. As she stood adrift, Connie Featherstone waved her over. Connie's full face was beet red as she fanned herself continuously with a serviette, seated next to a serene and unruffled Pierre sporting his monocle.

"We've two seats here," puffed Connie.

"Lovely!" said Imogen.

"Enchanté," Pierre purred, lifting his white Panama hat and glancing over Imogen's shoulder.

"How are you enjoying the fête so far?" Connie asked. "Pierre and I are both on the committee."

"Marvelous," Imogen replied. "We've enjoyed fresh chips from the fish and chip stand, sampled the local honey and jams and had fun running the egg and spoon race. The turnout is staggering. It seems as though everyone in the county has come."

"Alors, I think that's because of the Ferris wheel," said Pierre, stirring sugar into his tea. "The colonel is a forward thinker. I wasn't sure about it, but he was right, it is a draw."

"Well, Ophelia certainly enjoyed it."

"She took a ride? I'm too nervous," confessed Connie. "I'd rather keep my feet firmly on the ground."

"Me too," agreed Imogen.

"It's not bad," added Pierre. "I took a turn and found it rather exciting."

Imogen waved at Ophelia who threaded her way through the tables.

"Connie. Pierre." She plonked the tray down on the table and Imogen was thrilled to see two cream buns. "It's thirsty work running those races."

"I don't doubt it," said Pierre.

They spent the next twenty minutes in pleasant conversation, then Pierre glanced at his heavy, gold watch. "Duty calls." He pushed back his chair and doffed his hat.

"Isn't he lovely?" said Connie as they watched him leave. "So well-dressed and polite. He could teach the English men a thing or two."

"He certainly could," replied Ophelia, causing Imogen to examine her sister's features.

"It's a wonder he never married," continued Connie, her tone dreamy.

"I think there was someone once," said Ophelia taking a sip of her tea. "Or so I've heard."

Connie's forehead shone. "I think we'll have a lovely amount for the widows this year." She finished up the generous piece of Victoria sponge on her plate with a loud swallow. "Even after paying our expenses."

Imogen tucked into her cream bun, realizing that she had worked up quite an appetite.

"Where do we find the rope for the tug of war?" asked Ophelia. "That's what we're in charge of next."

"In the supply tent. But it's rather heavy," said Connie. "I'll come with you."

They finished their tea and headed back out into the pleasant summer sun. A few bilious clouds provided refreshing shade as they followed Connie. She flung back the canvas door on the supply tent and stopped short.

"Ahhh!"

The hair-raising scream turned Imogen's blood cold.

The sisters pushed past Connie, to find the crumpled figure of the young journalist, Lila Winterbourne, lying lifeless on top of the thick rope.

# Chapter 8

Pushing past the hysterical Connie, Ophelia stepped forward, crouched and placed her fingers on the girl's neck. She shook her head.

"She's dead. Fetch the constable."

Constable Hargrove was a solid man in his early forties with not much between the ears. He was perfect for the sleepy little village of Saffron Weald's usual problems, such as lost cats, or poached chickens, but Imogen feared he would be completely out of his league faced with an actual murder.

Hand over her mouth, Connie left, gasping great sobs, in search of the constable who was attending the fair in his official capacity.

"Ophelia, we both know the shortcomings of Constable Hargrove. I'll stand guard by the door while you search for clues."

Imogen stepped out of the tent and carefully pulled down the door flap. No one had reacted to Connie's scream because there were too many other squeals and shrieks from those on the Ferris wheel or winning prizes at the stalls. She attempted to look casual.

Her mind was spinning. Who would want to kill a young girl who wrote fluff for the county newspaper? Imogen was surprised to find that she was not panicked by the death. Instead, she felt her brain begin to process the grisly discovery with cool logic. *Who was she? Where in the county did she live? Had she worked at any other newspaper? Did she have a relationship with anyone in the village? Why was she in the supply tent? How long had she been dead?*

"How's it going?" Imogen whispered hoarsely through the canvas. She had no doubt that her sister was capable and not too squeamish, but when it came to detail, perhaps

Imogen was the better choice. She was certainly the more practical. Although, come to think of it, Ophelia had shown extreme levelheadedness recently.

"I've found a notebook in her shoulder bag and it is not—how shall I put it? What you might expect from our short association with her. It's full of notes she made *before* coming. And it's all about the people in the village. We're not listed, but mother is. I'm just scanning it. Wish I could take it home for a proper look."

"Oh, that wouldn't be right, lovey." Imogen was getting antsy that the constable would appear at any moment.

"I know. I'll put it back. Oh, look here! Some pages have been torn out."

Imogen heard the sound of her sister moving around then a gasp. "Here's a library card in the name of Willa Medford. I do believe she was here under false pretenses. She could be a common thief."

"How did she die?" asked Imogen.

"Looks like a swift bang on the back of the head with a wooden post. I bet she didn't even see it coming." There was more rustling as Ophelia crept hither and thither. "Just searching for more clues. There's a crushed, boiled sweet by the door. But that could've been left by anyone. Those things are everywhere and stick to the bottom of shoes. Oh, and there's a sequin stuck to the bottom of her right shoe."

"A sequin?" Imogen snapped her fingers. "There was a lady's dance troop who performed while we were having tea. They were wearing sequined jackets."

"There's an empty packet of French cigarettes in the corner," continued Ophelia, "and she has dried mud on the soles of her shoes."

"It hasn't been wet and muddy recently," whispered back Imogen.

"Good point," Ophelia agreed. More rustling. "Ooh, I found a crushed flower petal under her."

"Ophelia, lovey, I don't think you're supposed to move dead bodies before the police have seen them."

"I know. I just rolled her a quarter turn."

A wave of energy was fast approaching the tent.

"I think the constable is coming," called Imogen, urgently.

Ophelia appeared beside her, straightening her hat. Imogen glared at her sister's glove. Ophelia looked down and noticed a smudge of blood. *Hot crumpets!* She ripped off both gloves and stuffed them into her handbag just as Constable Hargrove appeared. Connie was nowhere in sight.

"Ladies," he said, his tone grim and his ruddy skin a nasty tint of green. "Miss

F-Featherstone has informed me that…" he could not finish the sentence. Instead, he tipped his head toward the tent door.

"Yes, Constable. My sister and I have been keeping guard. Would you like to go in?" Ophelia indicated the door flap as she and Imogen stepped aside.

The constable pulled a handkerchief from his pocket and wiped his lips. "Of course."

Telegraphing a message to her sister via eye contact, Imogen followed the policeman into the supply tent with Ophelia on her heels.

He stopped, staring at the poor girl, and stuffed the handkerchief to his mouth.

"Are we sure?"

"Oh, yes, Constable. I checked for a pulse as soon as we found her," explained Ophelia. "There's no hope."

He nodded, gulping in air, then vanished through the door faster than a magician, the sounds of heaving betraying him. By tacit agreement, Ophelia stood at the door this time, and Imogen went straight for the girl's bag. Items in it included the library card, a tube of lipstick, a brush, and a coin purse. Imogen opened it quickly. Several pennies, farthings, a half crown…and a tiny key. She slipped the key into her pocket without thinking, then flipped through the pages of the notebook.

The name of the village was written on the first page, then separate pages were dedicated to various members of their small community.

She stopped at her mother's name. Beatrice Harrington. A question was written. *Does Mrs. Harrington know what happened to my mother? Why did she not answer my last letter?* Lila was in correspondence with their mother? It was obvious she did not know that Mrs. Harrington had died. But it had been in the obituary section of the county newspaper. It was beginning to look like Lila did not work as a journalist at all, or that she was working on something of far more significance than the history of the village fête.

Imogen reflected back on the conversation they had with the young girl before the fête began. She had not asked their names, and clearly was not on familiar enough terms with their mother to know she had twin girls. They must look to see if her mother had a letter from Miss Lila Weatherbourne, or rather, Miss Willa Medford.

Imogen flicked on. Pierre Ancien. Lila had written, *When did he arrive in the village? What did he do before opening an antique store in Saffron Weald?*

There was a page on Reginald. *Mr. Tumblethorne was born in the village which means he lived here in 1908.*

On the next page was an observation. *There is an underbelly of evil in this village.*

Evil? In sleepy, Saffron Weald! What *was* the girl investigating? Her thoughts pulled up short. What if her inquiries led to her murder?

Imogen flicked on. Bartholomew Cresswell. The vicar! *Find out what he did in the war.*

Imogen wasn't even sure the vicar had served in the war. He would have been in his early thirties. *When did he come to Saffron Weald?*

Arabella and Fred Fudgeford. *They have not lived here long enough.* "For what?" thought Imogen. *Where did they live before that?*

Mildred Chumley. *Busybody who may know important things she doesn't even realize. Lived here at the right time.*

Ophelia cleared her throat rather loudly, and Imogen slipped the notebook back into the girl's bag and stepped beside her sister as the hapless policeman reappeared, looking much worse for wear. He reentered the tent, keeping his eyes on the twins rather than the corpse.

"There's bound to be a county doctor in the first aid tent," said Ophelia. "He could make an inventory of the body, declare the cause of death, which I believe is a blow to the head, and arrange for the removal of the poor girl."

Constable Hargrove wiped his fevered brow. "I think that might be for the best." He lunged for the door, and Imogen could already imagine herself looking through the notebook again.

"Constable!" It was a deep male voice.

*Dash my dahlias! Too late!*

An older man poked his head into the tent. "Miss Featherstone directed me over here. I'm Dr. Pemberton." The doctor dropped his voice. "Something about a murder?"

The constable murmured, something incomprehensible and passed outside as the doctor entered.

"Ladies," he said, touching his hat. "What have we here?"

# Chapter 9

As the sisters sat in the kitchen, the sinking sun dousing the room with amber tinted light, they gathered their thoughts and observations on paper.

"I've got Mother, Pierre, the vicar, the Fudgefords and Mildred," said Imogen. "Who am I missing?

The fête had closed down an hour early. There had been no grand announcement about the murder, since Lila was not a local. When the constable had recovered his senses and spoken to the colonel, they had concluded that such an announcement would only cause unnecessary panic which was to be avoided at all costs. Quiet, one-on-one requests that the stalls close early due to the fear of inclement weather was enough. Only the Ferris wheel operator made a fuss and he was paid in full on the spot, which earnings he promptly took over to the Dog and Whistle.

"You also mentioned Reginald on the way home," added Ophelia. "And in my quick look I saw a page on the Puddingfields and the colonel himself."

"It makes quite a list." Imogen underlined her mother's name. "We need to check mother's desk for a letter from the girl."

The desk was an antique bought by their grandmother from the reign of Charles I. In need of some tender care, it wore spots from hot teacups like wounds from war and one of the legs was wobbly. Each drawer had an elegant brass handle which was in need of a good buffing.

Ophelia opened the top drawer while Imogen sat on the windowsill beside the desk, watching. The drawer vomited forth old bills of sale and receipts. Having carefully examined them, it was clear there was no correspondence.

"One day we should check the dates and throw them all away, but for now I give you permission to stuff them all back where they came from," said Imogen.

"Good because you know how I hate filing things," Ophelia replied.

She opened the second drawer. It was full of what could only be described as disorganized junk.

"Mother was more like you than I realized," chuckled Imogen.

Old pens that no longer worked, paper clips, erasers, old ink bottles. A morass of catastrophic proportions.

"Let's check the bottom drawer and only go through that mess if we come up blanks."

"Agreed," said Imogen, holding her breath.

The last drawer was almost impossible to open. Chock full of papers, documents and letters. Ophelia pulled out a paper from the middle of the pile.

"It's a letter from Granny dated 1877. The script is beautiful."

"What's it about?" asked Imogen.

Ophelia ran an eye over the copper plate handwriting. "It's the response to something mother had written to her. She must have had some questions about raising adolescent girls." She brought the page closer. "*I am sure Ophelia will grow out of her bad skin. Send her into the fresh air for long country walks. That should do the trick.*"

"I don't remember you having pimply skin," Imogen mused.

"That's because yours was smooth as porcelain. I used to complain to mother all the time. How could we be identical twins and have such different complexions?"

"True. I was lucky."

"Ooh, here's a bit about you. *If you give Imogen poetry to read, she is sure to come out of her funk. Try Shelley and Longfellow.*"

Imogen smiled at the memory. "I was ravenously reading gothic romance novels and had no time for anything else. It was so unlike real life romance that I probably did get a bit depressed. How old were we?"

"Fifteen."

"A dreadful age. I spent hours mooning under the willow or wrapped up on the big sill on the stairs. I do remember Mother trying to ply me with poetry but I had no time for it."

"I read them all," said Ophelia. "Poetry spoke to my soul."

She placed the letter on the top of the desk and started at the top of the haphazardly filed pile. It wasn't until she was three quarters of the way through that she found what they were looking for.

"Bingo! Two letters from Willa Medford. Evidence that is her real name." She flattened the first on the top of the desk and Imogen came to stand beside her.

*February 5, 1928*
*Wisteria Cottage,*
*West Wallop, Wiltshire*
*Dear Mrs. Harrington,*

*I am writing to you in the hopes that you may have some information that would help me in the quest to discover what happened to my mother. She died when I was a baby and I have recently come into possession of some old notes of hers that call into question everything I thought I knew.*

*I was told by my grandmother, who raised me, that she died of the flu in 1908 and had no reason to question it. My father died in an accident before I was born.*

*Recently, my grandmother also passed away and as I was going through some of her things, I found a notebook belonging to my mother. It appears that Mother believed that someone she had crossed paths with had committed a murder and got away with it. In her notes, she details that she told all this to a policeman who said he would look into it. He never did.*

*I think my mother followed the murderer to Saffron Weald and began asking questions, posing as a journalist for a women's magazine. That was 1908, the year she supposedly died of the flu.*

*I fear the murderer killed my mother to cover up their original crime.*

*I came across your name and address in her notebook. I am hoping you can help me.*

*Awaiting your response,*
*Willa Medford.*

"Well!" exclaimed Imogen. "Mother never spoke to me on the subject."

"Me neither! How extraordinary! But this might explain why Willa was pretending to be a journalist."

"What does the other letter say?" asked Imogen.

Ophelia placed the second letter on top of the first and noticed that something was attached to the back. Pulling off the paper clip, they gasped. It was an old sepia photograph of a woman in a long skirt and shirtwaist, with familiar, frizzy hair and downturned eyes.

"Lila, or Willa rather, is the spitting image of her mother," declared Ophelia.

Imogen took the photograph and traced the edges with her finger as her sister read the second letter.

*April 3, 1928*
*Wisteria Cottage,*
*West Wallop, Wiltshire*
*Dear Mrs. Harrington,*

*Thank you for replying to my letter. I am enclosing a photograph of my mother. Perhaps you recognize her?*

*I am more convinced than ever that my mother was on the trail of a murderer who killed her to keep their identity a secret.*

*As a resident of the village perhaps you can wheedle information out of the residents without letting the cat out of the bag. I am looking for someone who lived in or visited Wiltshire before 1908 and also lived in Saffron Weald after that time.*

*I am afraid the police will not take me seriously unless I have concrete proof of their guilt.*
*I await any insight you might find out.*
*Willa.*

Ophelia dropped the letter onto the desk. "It's dated a month before Mother died. That's why she didn't respond to Willa's letter. The girl must have decided to take matters into her own hands when she got no response and came to the fête incognito. A public event should have been safe.

"But either the murderer spotted and recognized her since she looks so like her mother, or she confronted them and they panicked."

"So, what do we do now?" asked Imogen.

"This person has killed twice," replied Ophelia. I doubt they will suddenly get a conscience about killing a third time. I think we must be very careful."

"You sound like me!"

"Do you disagree?" asked Ophelia.

"No! I'm not ready to shuffle out of this earthly existence just yet. Do we owe Willa anything? I think maybe we just let the police do their job."

"Really? Aren't you just the teensiest bit curious? I didn't mean to suggest that we wash our hands of it at the first sign of danger," contradicted Ophelia. "Mother clearly thought it a worthy cause. And it might be fun."

Imogen widened her eyes. "Fun?"

"You like mystery books. Why?"

Imogen's neck sank into her shoulders. "Because it's so satisfying. There's a crime, clues, an investigation and a clever resolution."

"Think how much more satisfying it would be to put a real criminal behind bars."

Imogen's face squashed into contempt. "Fun with a large side of personal danger!"

"All I'm saying is, we keep our eyes and ears open, ask pertinent questions every now and again and use our collective intellect to draw conclusions. If we feel the least threatened, we can refrain."

Imogen huffed and rested her cheek on her fist. "Perhaps I should recruit Fergus. He's a levelheaded and logical thinker."

"No!" cried Ophelia. "If your children get the slightest whiff of this, they'll haul us out of here quicker than you can say *hot crumpets*."

Imogen smirked. "I daresay you're right, lovey."

"I am!" replied Ophelia with vigor. "I think we play it low key but consider everything that goes on here through the lens of this mystery. I think it's our duty to rid this tranquil village of a wickedly bad apple. We deserve to live out our days in peace and safety. If this village is harboring a killer, we owe it to everyone to expose them. And frankly, Hargrove's not up to the job."

Imogen pursed her lips. "It rather bursts the innocence of the old place, don't you think?"

"The murderer did that by killing a lovely young thing in her prime. He must not be allowed to escape justice."

"If you say so."

Ophelia began pacing the room, the light of inspiration in her eyes. "From here on out, we must be on our guard with everyone."

"Everyone?" asked Imogen, her chest pricked with concern.

"Well, not everyone. Let me think. Willa's mother came here twenty years ago. So, anyone under the age of forty should be off the hook."

Imogen's lips twisted. "That means we must suspect most of our friends."

"Unfortunately, that's correct, ducky."

"How should we proceed?" asked Imogen tapping the arm of the chair and watching her sister wear out the already threadbare rug.

"How about we quietly announce what the colonel told us; that mother was writing a history of the village from the time of Elizabeth I and that we want to finish up what she started? As a longtime member of the historical society, it was a natural thing for her to do, and for us to want to complete. We can say we want to publish it for locals and as a tourist book that can be sold at the pub, the antique shop or anywhere else. That will give us permission to search through history books in the library and ask questions without raising suspicions."

"Alright, that is a good idea but I've been thinking," said Imogen. "I think the police will send an inspector to help Hargrove. What if he solves the crime in the meantime?"

"I have no doubt that the higher ups *will* send an inspector to work this case. But who knows if he will be any good? But, if they *do* catch Willa's killer, we can still piece together the older murder and bring Willa's mother some justice."

# Chapter 10

Sitting together on their old pew, dressed in Sunday best, the sisters listened as Reverend Cresswell gave a rousing sermon on loving one's neighbor. The grapevine had done its work and everyone in Saffron Weald knew there had been a murder of a stranger. The church was overflowing.

"Have you recovered?" Imogen asked Connie in fellowship hall after the service.

The librarian's eyes bulged behind the heavy frames. "No! I keep seeing the poor girl's blank stare. Makes my blood run cold. I'm even considering getting a guard dog."

Connie Featherstone was a spinster who preferred cats. But felines were no protection against intruders.

"I made Marmaduke sleep on my bed last night. At least he could alert me to danger rather than leaving me to be killed in my sleep. But I didn't get a wink."

Though murder was, by definition, a personal crime, the rippling effects of terror on a small community like Saffron Weald, were extremely public. All the while the murderer was still at large, no one felt safe.

"I'm glad Ophelia and I have each other," remarked Imogen. "Especially since we have decided not to get a pet."

"Do you really think you two could defend yourself against a killer at your age?"

Ophelia swallowed down her pride. "Two brains against one are always better odds."

"I suppose so." Connie wiped her nose with a purple handkerchief. "But I've made up my mind. I'm going to the county pound first thing tomorrow. I'm looking for an Alsatian."

Imogen was of the opinion that Connie's response was knee-jerk but she held her tongue.

"Have you heard from Hargrove again?" Ophelia asked.

"I think he's even more nervous about it all than me, frankly," replied Connie. "The colonel intimated that an inspector would arrive today, but I haven't seen him."

"No doubt he would want to question us," said Ophelia. "And you, Connie."

Connie's features tightened with alarm. "I don't know if I can relive it all again. And I didn't stay like you two. No, I'll refer him to you."

As the women chatted, the colonel approached. "Morning, ladies."

Imogen indicated the empty chair next to her. "Have a seat, Colonel."

Usually, the colonel was serious but positive. This morning his jowls were drooping.

"Is there any news on the—unfortunate incident?" asked Imogen.

"Might as well call it what it is," he pronounced, placing his leather gloves on the table next to his coffee cup. "Murder."

Connie shivered, her salt and pepper curls trembling under a hideous red hat.

"Have you learned anything new?" persisted Imogen.

The colonel's prominent eyebrows formed a 'v'. "This is strictly on the Q.T, but we have reason to believe the girl had come here under false pretenses."

Connie's cup clattered onto the saucer. "What do you mean?"

The colonel lowered his voice. "I mean that she was not who she said she was. Not cricket that. Not cricket at all."

"You mean she wasn't Lila Weatherbourne?" said Ophelia, her face all innocent ignorance.

"No," replied the colonel. "We found a library card from Wiltshire in her bag bearing the name Willa Medford."

"Really?" said Ophelia. Imogen looked into her coffee cup.

"It was an easy thing for Constable Hargrove to track down the head librarian's telephone number and verify that information."

"On a Saturday evening?" asked Connie, apparently aware that she would not be at work herself over the weekend.

"Hargrove called her home number and asked her to go to the library and search the records but there was no need. West Wallop, Wiltshire is a small village and the librarian was personally acquainted with the victim. A brief description was enough to make a positive preliminary identification. The girl has no family, but the librarian gave the name of a friend who can come and make a formal identification."

"Oh, that is sad," said Imogen.

"Sad or not, what was the girl doing here? She said she was writing a piece on the history of the fête for the county rag. She even interviewed me on the subject, which was most inconvenient as I was spinning all manner of plates before the fête began."

"We could call and see if she worked for the newspaper in any capacity," said Connie.

"Wrong county," pointed out Imogen. "Lila, or Willa, is from Wiltshire, it would appear."

"A history of the fête?" commented Ophelia seizing on the topic to quietly introduce their latest venture. "Since we spoke to you about it, Colonel, Imogen and I have decided to continue mother's dabble in to writing a history of the village. Something worthwhile to sink our teeth into now that we are officially retired."

"Jolly good idea!" declared the colonel.

"We don't want to make a big fuss about it," clarified Imogen.

"I didn't know Beatrice was doing that," said Connie, stirring the tea in her cup. "Have you found her notes?"

Ophelia dunked a biscuit. "No. Hopefully, they'll appear during the redecorating."

"I could look out some textbooks for you," said Connie, helpfully. "Are you thinking of beginning with the village's origins?"

"Yes. A sort of timeline book. The kind tourists might find interesting. It could be sold at the shops and the pub."

"Sounds splendid." The colonel's mien had improved as the conversation had drifted away from the murder. "Not too many villages as old as ours that have maintained their original features. Not that we haven't had to fight for it," he added.

"I think that would be an important part of the book." Ophelia told them about the time their mother had taken them to protest.

"Your mother was a staple of the village," the colonel sighed. "Each passing is a scab on the old place that can't be healed."

"Oh-oh!" murmured Connie. "Don't look now but Mildred is coming."

"I'll be off then. Loads to do," declared the colonel, jumping to his feet and almost knocking over the chair in his haste to escape. "Afternoon, ladies."

As soon as he left, Mildred claimed his seat. Normally, the sisters would feel as he did, but gossipers might let slip things that would help in solving mysteries.

"Can you believe it?" declared Mildred, leaning across the table. "A murder!" She elongated the first syllable as if she were reading for the witch in Macbeth.

Imogen bit her lip. Murder was no laughing matter.

"As I hear it, the girl was an imposter. Perhaps she deserved to die," announced Mildred.

"Mildred!" cried Imogen. "No one deserves to be murdered. What a terrible thing to say."

Mildred withdrew her hands from the table as if Imogen had bitten them. "I'm just saying that she might have been a criminal herself. A wolf in sheep's clothing, so to speak."

"I think we should be careful about throwing stones until we know more," warned Ophelia. "Perhaps she had good reason to come incognito. Perhaps she knew the murderer, knew they were dangerous and was trying to protect herself."

Mildred pushed out her fleshy lips. "Perhaps. But liars are asking for trouble, in my humble opinion."

"What makes me nervous is that there is a murderer among us," said Connie, looking as though he might strike at any moment. "I had to talk myself into coming to church this morning."

"So glad to see you here," said the vicar, appearing at their table. "I hope you enjoyed this morning's message."

"Very timely, Vicar," said Imogen.

"I'm not sure there has ever been a murder in Saffron Weald," he continued. "Not a good precedent."

"Imogen and I have decided to embark on a history of the village. A short, pithy timeline book for tourists and villagers alike." She threw a look in her sister's direction. "Who knows? We may find that this is *not* the first murder."

Connie gripped the table, white knuckles showing. "Oh, please no!" she pleaded. "Let's have no more talk of murder."

"Vicar, did you know the girl's real name was Willa Milford," asked Mildred, as though she were a cat presenting him with a dead mouse.

"Medford," said Ophelia before she could stop herself, and flashed worried eyes at Imogen.

"How do *you* know?" asked Mildred.

"The colonel mentioned it," said Ophelia.

"Did you know they were with me when I found the body," said Connie. "It shook me to the core, I can tell you.

They stayed with the poor girl while I went to fetch the constable."

"Were you?" purred Mildred, eyes full of a macabre interest that made Imogen shiver.

"It was terrible," responded Ophelia.

"There is some talk that she was from a village in Wiltshire," added the vicar. "West Wallop. I know because I grew up in the village next door."

# Chapter 11

All the way home, the twin sisters discussed the bizarre revelation that the vicar had grown up in the Wiltshire village next to West Wallop.

"I don't like the presence of coincidences when the stakes are so high," declared Imogen. "And the vicar *is* in the right age group."

"*Flaming fiddles*! You're seriously considering him as a suspect?" Ophelia snapped her fingers. "He only moved here a few years ago."

Imogen flattened her lips. "He could have been visiting in 1908. We didn't live here then but we came quite often."

Ophelia sighed. "Alright. Reverend Cresswell, suspect number one."

"We've got to start somewhere, lovey."

They hurried up the garden path, eager to record things in their notebook. Ophelia grabbed Puccini, laid it on the gramophone and leaned back in her chair, fingers forming a pyramid.

"Puccini helps me think."

Imogen rolled her eyes. Between their mother's passion for opera, and her sister's, she had been subjected to the strains of it her whole childhood as they sang whole sections at the top of their lungs. Her father had not been a fan either and the two of them would steal away to the garden for some peace.

With the invention of the gramophone, her poor father had been subjected to it daily and had suddenly become a regular at the *Dog and Whistle*.

"Just one side then, lovey. We don't all appreciate opera like you do."

Imogen added the vicar's name to the notebook and underlined it as her sister meditated. She thought of her husband, good steady Wilfred. What would he do next?

She chewed the pencil. He would consider the list in order. Methodically.

"Connie. What do we know about her?" Imogen began.

"Quite a lot since we all went to school together. Constance was born in the village like us. She was an only child. Lived with her parents until they both died and then became the sole resident of their cottage."

"Golly. That sounds terribly boring. Has she *never* left?" Imogen asked this question with her pencil hovering next to Connie's name.

"I don't think so," said Ophelia. "But we should find out. Put a question mark next to her name."

"Already done. Did she never have a beau?"

Ophelia closed her eyes again as the annoying music hit a crescendo. "I have a vague memory that she was seeing someone back in 1884. Can't remember what happened to him or why they never married."

"I'll add that as a question," said Imogen. "Pierre is next."

"Hmmm. Pierre. When did he move here? Not till 1895, I think. But the first murder was in 1908. That means he was here then."

"What do we know of *his* past?" asked Imogen.

Ophelia looked to the left, fingers to her lips. "Let me think. Has he ever mentioned where he was born?" She snapped her fingers. "La Vendée! I remember him mentioning it once. Do you recall we went there on holiday one year? That's why I remember."

"Not really. Does he have any family?"

"A sister and a brother who still live in France. He visits them from time to time."

"What was his profession?" Imogen ploughed on.

"Before becoming an antique dealer? I don't know. Perhaps he has always dealt in antiques."

Imogen noticed that Ophelia was brushing at lint on her flowing skirt. "We can ask next time we see him. Righty-ho! Who's next?"

"The vicar, who we now know is from Wiltshire, to wit, the village next to West Wallop." Imogen lifted her head. "Isn't that such a fun name for a village?"

Ophelia grinned. "I have to hide a smile each time someone says it. What else do we know about him?"

"Not much. I have no idea where his wife is from or where he started his clerical life. I bet Mildred would know about all that."

"Very possibly. But that would mean we have to invite her to tea or something. I don't know if I have the stomach for it."

"No," agreed Imogen. "But needs must, and all that. I suppose we could visit with his wife." She looked back at the list. "The Fudgefords. How old do you think they are?"

"I have trouble guessing people's ages these days. They all look so young."

"Arabella is definitely younger than my Penny which might make her outside our age range. That strikes them both off." Imogen drew the pencil through their names. "Reginald Tumblethorn is next."

"Can you see dear Reggie killing anyone?" asked Ophelia. "I remember how heartbroken he was when his cat died."

"I shall need to act as devil's advocate here, then," said Imogen. "I think we cannot make assumptions or give in to our preconceptions."

Ophelia sat up. "*Blazing bagpipes!* Look at *you* taking on the detective role after wobbling at the start! And you're absolutely right! We need to put our assumptions aside and look at the facts."

"Reginald fits the age group *and* he lived in the village twenty years ago."

"It would be easy enough to chat to him in the shop. He's no Mildred but he's not averse to a bit of gossip. If we bring up the murder, he's sure to take the bait."

Imogen wrote a note next to his name to bring up the murder on their next trip to the grocer's. "Next are the Puddingfields. They are old enough and they have lived in Saffron Weald at least as long as we Harringtons."

"Yes, they have. What else do we know about them? Didn't they have a son who died at the Somme?" asked Ophelia.

"I believe so. I understand they also have a daughter who would be in her thirties. I don't think she lives in the village."

Ophelia began to hum along to the music as Imogen kept writing. "Though Alice Puddingfield hales from Brighton, she's lived here for the last forty years so that fits our window too."

"I know we set the standard of removing assumptions, but Alice, really?" remarked Ophelia.

"You can't bend the rules for anyone," Imogen reminded her.

"I suppose you're right," responded Ophelia with a large sigh. "Anyone else?"

Imogen cleared her throat. "The colonel."

"Ha, ha! Good job you reminded me of the rule," said Ophelia with a sly grin. "Born here and now retired here. Whether it has been more than twenty years, I have no idea."

"Should be easy enough to find out," remarked Imogen.

The music had stopped and the regular catch of the needle punctuated their conversation. Ophelia rose to stop it.

"First, I think a visit to the library will give us fodder to launch from when we talk to people. Are you up for that tomorrow?" asked Imogen.

The village library was situated on the south side of the pond and was originally built as a small schoolhouse. However, when lending libraries became widespread at the end of the nineteenth century, the nobleman of the time had suggested building a larger schoolhouse for the growing population and transforming the old building into a library. Though the villagers at the time saw no particular need for literacy, they were all for someone paying for an upgrade and agreed.

In keeping with the rest of the buildings in the village, the library was built in the wattle and white daub style with a central chimney. Since its creation, the library had received at least three, hotly debated additions, and as a consequence was a rather odd shape. Defying the laws of gravity, none of the outside walls were plumb and the front peak positively bulged forward causing the leaded window to lean at a perilous angle.

As the twins stepped through the original, cross-beamed barn door, and onto the rutted floor, they were greeted by the familiar scent of old books mingled with the faint aroma of smoke which became embedded into the very fiber of the books each winter.

Polished oak bookshelves took up every inch as far as the eye could see except for the checkout desk at the back of the original building. One extension was devoted to children's literature and the other to adult fiction. The main room of the library housed all the non-fiction titles.

They stepped past stacks of non-fiction, to the librarian's desk at the rear which enjoyed a small halo of light from the back windows. Connie had her head down over a pile of neatly stacked papers which shared the desk with antique brass lamps and china cat statues.

Ophelia cleared her throat and Connie looked up, eyes bloodshot, her hair disheveled.

"Oh, hello," she responded, putting a hand to her hair self-consciously.

"Still not sleeping?" asked Imogen.

"Can you tell?"

"Hardly," lied Ophelia. "You had just mentioned it after church."

Connie rubbed her eyes and Imogen wanted to pull her fists away. Everyone knew women should not tug at the fine skin under them.

"I need toothpicks just to keep my eyes open and I jump every time someone comes in the door." She looked up through a veil of fatigue. "What can I do for you?"

They reminded her of their new 'project' to continue their mother's history of the village.

"Oh, right. Look, I haven't had a chance to pull any books for you but if you go to the third stack from the front door, on the left side is our history collection."

"We're big girls, ducky," said Ophelia. "We can figure it out."

"Great," said Connie, slumping back into her chair. "Have at it."

They found the correct location and began scouring the book spines.

"I think we should begin twenty years ago and go backward," Ophelia whispered.

"Agreed." Imogen stopped her finger on a large book about Meadowshire through the ages and pulled it down. There was no room for tables and chairs in the little library except in the children's section, so she leaned against the bookshelf and opened the heavy tome.

The foreword described the title as an overview of the county since the Middle Ages. She flipped to the index and found three references to the village. The first was about a knight of Henry IV who built a large estate where the current nobleman lived. That structure was long gone but he had employed people to farm his land and built small cottages at the bottom of the rise, the cottages that still stood today. The second article was about a witch trial that was held in the mid-1700s where a local feudal farmer's wife was suspected of being a witch and dipped into the pond to see if she survived.

*Barbaric! She probably just had a mind of her own.*

The third mention of Saffron Weald was from 1908. Imogen's heart skipped. She flicked to the correct page.

*"In the spring of 1908 a young, female, name unknown, was found dead in the forest below Stirling Manor. She had been dead for several months by the time she was found, which made identification difficult, and the doctor concluded she had fallen on the slope and hit her head on a rock. An inquest delivered a verdict of death by misadventure."*

At the end of the article was a scratchy black and sepia picture of a woman's body face down.

"Look at this." Imogen showed her sister the open book. They swapped volumes.

Ophelia's was a digest of famous people with roots in the county.

Imogen flicked straight to the index.

The colonel was listed, as was Connie's grandfather who had apparently created a patent for knee length rubber boots. This was news to Imogen. A much older date, 1723, listed Algernon Bristlethwaite as secretary to the Prime Minister.

Imogen thumbed her way to the page about the colonel.

*Horatio Winstanley, son of Horace Winstanley, educated at Easton Priory Public school was distinguished in the second Boer War for bravery under fire and received a Victoria Cross for saving his men in battle. Receiving a battlefield promotion, Winstanley was promoted from*

*Brigadier to Colonel and received his medal from the hand of Queen Victoria herself before her death in 1901.*

Nothing of value to their investigation here. Imogen vaguely wondered if his name was engraved on the war memorial on the edge of the village green.

"Confirmation of Willa's query," said Ophelia, bringing Imogen back from her thoughts. "But *she* does not believe it was an accident. Well done! Shall I be the scribe for this?"

Imogen handed her the new notebook they had bought for their 'research'. "Who knows? Perhaps we really will end up writing a book."

"In that case, you can put that the colonel and Connie's grandfather are local celebrities." She related the relevant facts and Ophelia wrote them down with the bibliographies.

They pushed the books back and continued scouring.

Ophelia stopped her search at a book called *Mysteries of Meadowshire County*.

The index of chapters showed that the book was divided into decades. She flipped to 1900. There had been a ghost sighting near the pond, a theft of some silver candlesticks from the church, an eclipse of the sun…and the discovery of an unidentified body.

*While conducting his regular circuit of the Stirling estate, the viscount's steward came upon the body of a young woman at the bottom of the rise, partially hidden by bushes. Blood matted in her hair indicated she had hit her head as she fell down the embankment. Advanced decomposition made identifying the body impossible.*

*After making discreet enquiries around the village and other local villages and hamlets in the county, no one came forward to identify the woman. Her identity remains a mystery to this day, as does the reason for her visit to Saffron Weald.*

Ophelia made notes then handed the book to her sister.

"I think we should visit the library in West Wallop to look through their archived newspapers and dig about for more background on Willa," suggested Imogen.

"Me too."

"Find everything you needed?" Ophelia almost dropped the book she was holding as Connie surprised them.

"Yes, thank you," they both replied.

"I think we have enough to begin a framework. We'll come back as necessary," added Imogen. "How did we not know that your grandfather patented rubber goloshes?"

Connie's expression slipped to bashful. "Well, he didn't actually patent the boots. Some American chap did that with tyre rubber in 1852. Granddad added the cotton interior to keep feet warm. But yes, we're very proud of him."

Imogen thought of the modest cottage Connie had inherited from her parents.

"I know what you're thinking," said Connie. "Where's the money? Well, my uncle, Desmond, had a gambling habit and *poof*! It was all gone in a moment."

"Did he live in Saffron Weald?"

"No," replied Connie. "He went to London to seek his fortune and returned a pauper."

# Chapter 12

Peter Cleaver was arriving to mow the lawn as the twins departed for a day in West Wallop. They took a taxi to Parkford station to catch the train to Salisbury. From there they would look for a bus or take another taxi.

It was a beautiful day, but one never knew in England, so they each took an umbrella which served double duty as a walking stick if they needed the extra balance after a long day on their feet. The train station at Parkford was a county hub with trains connecting to London and the southeast coast and even as far north as Birmingham. As they waited on platform three, they caught sight of the colonel, smartly dressed in tweed on platform five. Ophelia tried to get his attention but his head was in the Times. She checked the train board. Platform five was going to London.

Their train whistled into the station like a gleaming snake and the sisters hopped aboard. They had not splurged on a first-class ticket as they reasoned that a train to Salisbury would not be overcrowded. They were wrong. They walked along the corridor looking into compartments that bulged with humanity, feeling more depressed as they progressed.

"Perhaps passengers will descend at Ramsford," said Imogen. "There are a lot of shops there. We can wait it out in the restaurant."

Thankfully, the restaurant car was almost empty and they found a table for two with a white tablecloth and single, plastic flower in a thin vase.

A waiter approached, his hair oiled more than a racing car at Brooklands Racing Circuit. His start betrayed his surprise. "Afternoon ladies. What can I get for you?"

Ophelia recognized the severe tones of an east London accent. "I'll take a cup of tea and a sticky bun, please."

"Make that two," added Imogen.

"Ha!" guffawed the lad. "Crikey! You look like two peas in a pod *and* you order the same thing."

The sisters were not unused to the comments of strangers. There was a time in their adolescence when they had gone out of their way to style themselves differently, but as they aged, they would laugh, upon meeting, to find that they had chosen the same color frock, though Ophelia's were always more whimsical.

"Where should we begin in West Wallop?" asked Imogen. "The pub?"

"Not a bad idea. That or a tea shop. And I don't think we should betray where we're from, since the papers have reported the murder now. We can say we're from Chipping Harcross in Oxford if we're asked, and we're out for the day. We recognized the village name from the news articles and thought we'd take a look."

"Won't that make us seem like the worst of busybodies?" asked Imogen.

"We'll never see these people again, so it doesn't really matter, does it, ducky?"

"I suppose not."

The waiter returned with their tea and buns and Ophelia paid him. The bun was sticky but not very fresh, but what could one really expect on a country train line?

The train pulled into Ramsford, and the sisters watched as a lot of passengers descended with only one or two stepping aboard.

"That should have let up some room," said Ophelia.

They found an empty carriage and settled in. Imogen withdrew a book and Ophelia looked out of the window, enjoying the bucolic landscape before being rocked to sleep by the train.

Imogen shook her awake. It took Ophelia a second to realize where she was. "We'd better be quick or the train will head off with us still aboard," warned Imogen.

Gathering her wits and brushing off the tendrils of sleep, Ophelia stood and the sisters descended onto the large, bustling platform. With its lovely cathedral, Salisbury was a prominent city in Wiltshire.

"If we have time, I'd love to look at the cathedral, Ophelia."

"My orchestra performed there once," Ophelia replied. "Excellent acoustics. Yes. Let's see if we have time." She led the way to the ticket counter. "Excuse me, what is the best way to West Wallop? Bus or taxi?"

"There's a bus goes right to the village green." The man looked at his watch. "If you hurry, you might just make it."

"Thank you."

They bustled outside and found the bus at the stop about ready to leave. Madly waving it down, they hopped aboard.

"Phew, that was a bit of luck," said Imogen, slamming into her seat.

"West Wallop," said Ophelia when the conductor approached. "How far is it?"

"Twenty minutes," he said, his eyes snapping from one twin to the other. "I'll let you know when we arrive."

The bus pulled through the city and onto a wide country road which narrowed every three miles or so until it could only generously be called a track.

"West Wallop!" cried the conductor.

The sisters arose and Imogen asked the time of the last bus back.

"Every hour until six o'clock," the conductor responded.

"That should do nicely. Thank you."

They looked around as the bus lumbered away. Saffron Weald was to picturesque, what West Wallop was to a worn out shoe. The village had none of the charm of Saffron Weald and it was obvious there was no active city council protecting its history. The buildings were a jumbled mess of architectural styles and the pub was an ugly, modern, concrete block called the *Pig and Trout*. Even the pond lacked charm.

Imogen's mouth pulled into an ugly shrug and Ophelia began her signature, silent laugh; shoulders shaking and tears appearing at the corners of her eyes.

"All English villages are not created equal," commented Imogen with raised brows.

Rejecting the soulless pub, they wandered along a short, winding high street and found a lackluster tea shop. Lace doilies had bred in excessive fashion and the grimy curtains were crocheted. The air held a mixture of mold and icing sugar. Imogen's nose wrinkled and Ophelia threatened to dissolve into another fit of laughter.

"Behave yourself, Ophelia."

A wiry girl with round spectacles and a mop of unruly blonde hair came from a door in the back. Her lips twitched at the sight of the two elderly copies. When she had recovered, she pointed to a little table by the window. "New round here, aren't you?" Her brogue was thick as toffee.

"Yes," replied Imogen who was the only one that could be trusted to speak at this moment. "We're out for a day in the countryside."

"And you chose West Wallop?" asked the girl, her head tilted in surprise.

Ophelia let slip a little snort and buried her head in her bag looking for a hankie.

"Well, it chose us really," replied Imogen. "We played a game and stuck a pin in a map and here we are."

"That's why you shouldn't leave things to chance," said the girl with a challenging frown.

"Yes, well, we're here now. What do you have on the menu?"

"Cook made flapjacks fresh this morning, there are vanilla fairy cakes from yesterday—I'd give those a pass, and custard tarts. Those aren't bad."

"Alright, we'll take two teas and a couple of custard tarts, please."

As she left, Ophelia's whole torso rocked with mirth. "Even the staff can't recommend the place!"

"I know. It does put rather a kink in our plans. Why would anyone come here?"

"I think we should stick to your brilliant story about the pin." Ophelia shook some more.

"It came to me in a flash of inspiration," responded Imogen.

"No one would come here otherwise," chortled Ophelia, considering using her handkerchief to wipe down the table before thinking better of it and placing it back in the bag.

"Honestly, lovey. Try to control yourself."

They looked out the window onto the bland street, with its blander shops and even Imogen couldn't stop a grin.

"Here you are!" The girl returned with a plain brown tray and began to lay a plate with the custard tarts on the table, then a non-descript pot and teacups.

"Does anything ever happen here?" asked Ophelia, sucking in her cheeks to try to stop herself from laughing. "I mean like a fête or a regatta?"

"We have Morris dancing and carry an effigy to the pond and chuck it in every May," the waitress replied, and Imogen had to avoid Ophelia's eye.

"How nice." Imogen took a quick bite of the tart and her face collapsed.

"As a village, it's a bit quiet. I'm leaving soon as I can. Trying to get a job in Salisbury," continued the waitress.

The bell over the door rang and a Dickensian farmer's wife, entered, her arms laden with baskets and a live chicken.

"Excuse me," said the girl and hurried off.

"Oh, my goodness!" declared Imogen. "This may have been a wild goose chase."

"It may end up as a wild chicken chase," said Ophelia eyeing the hen.

They munched half-way through the dry custard tarts and loaded the weak tea with sugar, then Ophelia waved to get the girl's attention.

"I thought of something," said the waitress, looking over her shoulder. "My cousin's, mother in-law's neighbor…" she dropped her voice. "Was murdered."

Ophelia dropped her cup. "What did you say, ducky?"

"A girl from this village was murdered in a place called Savage Wold."

Imogen began to correct her until she felt Ophelia's shoe connect with her shin.

"You don't say," replied Ophelia, making her eyes as round as possible. "What happened?"

"I heard it straight from my cousin. Her mother-in-law's neighbor was an old lady with a granddaughter about five years older than me. Maybe six. Anyway, the old lady died and left the house to the granddaughter. The girl was a bit mysterious but went on about finding something that meant her past was all a lie. The neighbor thought she might have been nipping at the whiskey, you know, with the grief, and all. Anyway, a few mornings ago, she left and didn't come back. The neighbor thought she was no better than she should be until yesterday, when a policeman came to ask her questions about the girl and explained that she was dead."

Ophelia brought her hand to her chest, her face a picture of shock. "I should say that was something, then. Did you know the girl?"

"No, more's the pity. She was older than me and I live on this side of the village and she lives on the other, round the pond and out half a mile. A little yellow place called Wisteria Cottage, with a bull for a weathervane, or so this cousin says. But it's something, eh?"

"It certainly is," said Imogen, reaching into her purse to pay the bill. "Do you have a library?"

Leaving the woman with the chicken, who was tucking into several fairy cakes, the two sisters left the tea shop and stood on the pavement. It had started to spit and they opened their umbrellas.

The library was a few yards down in a prefabricated hut. A sign on the door said it was closed until two. It was just on one.

"I think we should try and find Willa's house since this is closed," said Ophelia.

"Whatever for?" asked Imogen. "No one's there. It would be pointless."

"I think there's always something to be learned by seeing where someone lives, ducky. And besides, perhaps we can go in and have a look around."

"Are you mad? First of all, it's trespassing and secondly, it will be locked."

"You never know," replied Ophelia. "Come on. What else are we going to do for an hour?"

The cottage was, as the tea girl had said, a dull yellow with a ramshackle picket fence that was once white, and a bull weathervane. It was a single dwelling with the next neighbor at least fifty feet off.

Ophelia marched to the front door and tried the handle. *Locked.*

"See. A waste of time," declared Imogen with more than a little air of reproof.

"We'll see," said Ophelia reaching into her bag for something then flattening her body to the door.

82

"Voilà!"

The door swung open and Imogen's mouth did likewise. "How on earth…" Ophelia shuffled her in.

The dank air was stale with the smell of old fish.

Imogen hung by the door. "This feels wrong."

"Nonsense," replied Ophelia. "The girl is dead and we're trying to find out who did it."

The front door opened into a very cramped hall with a steep set of wooden stairs. On the left, Ophelia opened the door to a tiny sitting room. Moss green covers stretched over a sofa and two clumpy armchairs gathered around a pie crust coffee table. A miniscule black iron fireplace, cleaned of ashes, graced one wall. The curtains were closed, which made the room dim and Ophelia resisted the urge to fling them open. The room was tatty but neat as a pin.

"I'm going to the kitchen," Ophelia told her sister, who was still clinging to the front door.

Two steps farther down the hall was a tiny, old-fashioned kitchen. Lace curtains let in a little light and a sturdy table sat on curling linoleum.

"Eureka!" On the table, set out in rows, were diaries and papers.

Imogen's face popped around the door. "What?"

"Look, here's Mother's letter."

They each took a chair and Ophelia began to read,

*Badger's Hollow*
*Saffron Weald, Hampshire*
*February 7th, 1928*
*Dear Miss Medford,*
*Your letter took me quite by surprise. I hadn't thought of the woman you say is your mother, for years. I met her twice. The first time she approached me while I sat by the village pond feeding the ducks. She said she was writing an article for a women's magazine and asked if I had lived in the village for long. When I told her I had lived there all my*

*life, she became very interested and asked me about the villagers. I confess I was a little reluctant to tell a stranger the village secrets, so my descriptions were vague. At the conclusion of our interview, she gave me a handwritten card with her name on, and asked if she might call on me the next time she visited. I agreed, not expecting to ever see her again.*

*But a month later she returned and asked if anyone in the village had a connection to Wiltshire. I honestly did not know. We had a pleasant conversation about her baby and then we parted.*

*I'm sorry I can't be of more help,*
*Beatrice Harrington.*

"Mother spoke to Willa's mother!"

"Too bad Mother died before being able to help her. It might have prevented Willa's death."

Ophelia picked up a diary. She guessed by the old-fashioned flowing hand that it was Willa's mother's. Looking at the date, she saw it was from 1908.

*They found Albert Houndstooth in a well on his property today. They only knew it was him by the clothes he was wearing and his father's watch which was still in his pocket. Everyone believes it was a terrible accident but I am not so sure.*

*The doctor said he might have been down there a year or more given the decomposition of the body—he was a mere skeleton. But I remember someone asking about him in the village on market day— that were about a year ago. What if they killed him? I can't stop thinking that someone got away with murder and that I have the power to bring them to justice. I do remember they mentioned a place called Saffron Weald.*

*Mother won't listen to me, but I'm determined to see if I can do something about it.*

Another entry recounted how her mother thought she was becoming obsessed with her thoughts and told her that it was not good for the baby she was carrying, especially after losing her husband in an accident. Another page spoke of talking to the local constable but feeling that he didn't believe her. Then the entries changed and were all about Willa's birth, how happy she was and how the baby was healing the grief from losing her husband.

Ophelia flicked farther on as Imogen looked over her shoulder.

*I have found out how to get to Saffron Weald. It's not too far on the train. The baby is doing well and can be left with mother for one afternoon. I am going to tell mother I want to get some special fabric to make Willa a dress that I can only find in Salisbury. I am really going to talk to people in that village to see if I can't find the person who came to West Wallop that day then tell the police. It will ease my conscience. I am going tomorrow.*

Ophelia turned to the next page.

*Saffron Weald is a very pretty village. I talked to a few people but didn't learn much. I didn't see the person that came to West Wallop. I did meet a nice lady who has lived in the village her whole life. I described the person I was interested in, but she didn't recognize it as anyone in the village. She talked to me for quite some time but I had to get back to the station or I'd miss my train home. I feel as though I'm getting close, though. I'm going to go back again for one last try.*

"She did and it was the death of her," whispered Imogen.

*Knock, knock!*

The sisters froze.

# Chapter 13

A raspy, smoke polluted voice cried out, 'Hello?"

There was absolutely nowhere to run and Imogen thought she might have to vomit into her bag.

"Leave this to me," said Ophelia to Imogen then cried out, "In the kitchen!" as if she owned the place. She lowered her voice again as she swiped her mother's letters into her handbag. "If we demonstrate complete and utter confidence in our right to be here, who can challenge us?"

A tiny, squat woman with no teeth and a colorless scarf around steely hair, appeared in the doorway, hands on her hips. "What're you two doin' 'ere, then?" She squinted, closed her eyes and shook her head, then squinted at them again. "Don't often see that," she declared.

"I imagine not," said Ophelia with a smile, guiding the old lady back to the front door. "And we're here on official," she tapped the side of her nose, "business. Police business."

The rheumy gray eyes closed slightly. "This 'bout that poor girl getting 'erself killed? Wish she'd confided in me. I'd 'a warned 'er off. Never good to meddle in things where a murder is involved." The wrinkles of her face rearranged into a warning.

"You believed that her mother had been killed, then?" asked Ophelia as Imogen's heart rate began to descend from its mountain height.

"Well, now there, at first, I thought she was barkin'. You know how people get when a loved one dies. But when that policeman said Willa had been murdered, well, it got me to thinkin'. What if she were right about 'er mother's disappearance and the murderer killed 'er to keep 'er quiet? She was so young. Had 'er whole life ahead of 'er."

"So, the police have already questioned you?" asked Imogen, voice wobbling, heart rate spiking again. They had not considered the possibility that they might bump into an officer of the law on their field trip.

"Oh, yeah! Inspector somethin'. I didn't take to 'im, if you must know. Bit of a twit if you ask me. But I answered as well as I could. I owes it to Willa." She wiped her nose with a less than fresh hankie. "Give you the key, did they?"

"Yes. Constable Harbridge asked us to look around," replied Ophelia with authority, warning her sister with a look not to correct the constable's name. "As the only policeman in our village, he can't possibly do everything, you know."

"I'd a thought that inspector would do more," said the old lady.

"When was he here?" asked Ophelia.

"Yesterday a'ternoon. Asked me the same questions."

*Then why had he not taken the evidence from the table?* It suddenly struck Ophelia that the inspector might be coming back. *Drat!* She would have to return her mother's letters to the table and they would be obliged to leave pronto. Talking her way out of this sticky situation would be infinitely more difficult with an actual inspector and she had no desire to try it.

Another problem hijacked Ophelia's thoughts. If this nosy neighbor was interviewed again, she would be sure to tell the inspector about meeting the constable's elderly 'helpers'. She'd have to hope the inspector would put the neighbor's mention of twins in the cottage, down to the ravings of an old woman who was losing her marbles. Though Ophelia could tell the elderly neighbor was honestly as sharp as a tack. Time to move things along.

"Well, we've been asked to do some follow up. If you wouldn't mind…" Ophelia tipped her head to the front door.

"Of course. Can't be too sure, what with murderers on the loose. Needed to make certain no one was trying to break into Willa's cottage." She turned and began to reach for the front door handle.

"Did you know Willa's grandmother well?" asked Ophelia.

"Nigh on twenty year. Lovely woman. Bit nervy but she took great care of that baby. Raised 'er right."

"What about Willa's mother?"

The circular woman shook her head. "Not really. I moved in 'ere with my husband after she disappeared. Not that Willa's grandmother told me anything about that. She was very private. I think she was scared for the child." She turned to leave. "But you hear gossip."

After the neighbor left, Imogen let out a huge rush of air. "I don't know how you pulled that off, but you did. Shall we go? I don't want to risk the inspector coming back."

"I agree but not just yet. Remember that key you found in Willa's bag? Have you still got it? I'd like to find what it opens. You keep looking through the stuff on the kitchen table and I'll have a quick poke around upstairs."

"Sorry, lovey. I didn't even think about it."

"No matter. I'll figure something out." Ophelia left to climb the stairs.

Nerves dancing up her neck, Imogen kept a fretful eye on the time, then went back to the table. She could hardly concentrate and her gaze kept darting around the papers, unable to really settle on anything. There were a couple of local newspaper articles about the disappearance of Willa's mother. Nothing more.

Scraping sounds from upstairs now and again, made Imogen jump out of her skin. As she fingered aimlessly through the diary, she heard Ophelia shriek, "Bingo!", followed by hurried foot falls on the steep steps.

"Do be careful, lovey!" Imogen called.

Ophelia appeared in the kitchen, cheeks flushed and holding a small metal box with decorative inlay. "I am positive this is what the key opens."

"Too bad we don't have it," responded Imogen.

Ophelia took a hair pin from her bun and pulled it straight. "Never mind," she responded, wiggling the end of the pin in the tiny lock. "It's not a difficult one."

"Is that how you got in here?" asked Imogen. "I-I—"

"I got locked out several times over the years in London and became adept at picking the lock to my flat."

Imogen cleared her throat but said no more as the box sprung open. Inside were a couple of love letters from a young man, a lock of light hair, perhaps her mother's, and an old church bulletin from Saffron Weald dated 1908.

"Intriguing. This proves that Willa's mother *did* go to Saffron Weald. I'll just slip this bulletin into my pocket since the inspector didn't find the box. Finders keepers!"

"Is that proper?" asked Imogen, aghast.

"We can give it to him later if we deem it important. What about you?"

"Nothing new," replied Imogen, tapping her foot. "I really think we should leave."

"Well, what we've discovered tells us a lot more than we knew before." Ophelia glanced at her watch. "But you're right. It would be horribly awkward if the inspector arrived. I'll pop this box back under the bed." She ran up the stairs calling, "And if we leave now, we'll make it back to Salisbury in time to wander around the cathedral."

# Chapter 14

The one thing they had not found among the items at Willa's cottage, was a description of the person who had visited West Wallop right before Albert Houndstooth had disappeared.

*"That would have been far too easy and where's the fun in that?"* thought Ophelia as they ate a lazy breakfast after sleeping in.

Having made it to the cathedral in Salisbury well before closing, they had taken their time walking around and worn themselves out. As a consequence, they had both fallen asleep on the train and almost ended up in Dorset.

"That was one thing Wilfred and I could never agree on," declared Imogen as she buttered her toast. "He believed that sleeping in was a waste of precious time and I believe it is sometimes a necessary step for survival."

"Me too!" agreed Ophelia. "Orchestra members keep late hours. I'd often sleep till noon. Then practice till two, get a little water coloring done and be ready at the opera house at seven. Perfect for my internal clock."

"Hmm, well accountants are not artistic. They're purely practical creatures and that includes getting up at seven, rain or shine, weekday or weekend." Imogen drained her teacup. "And being discovered at Willa's cottage yesterday was absolutely terrifying. It totally drained me." She slathered the toast with jam. "But a good night's sleep was just the ticket. I propose we undertake something much kinder to my nerves, today— like shopping for furniture at Pierre's." She waved the butter knife at her sister. "But I haven't forgotten our mission. We can shop and ask our questions."

Ophelia huffed. "I suppose we do need to consider him, but I think it's silly."

Imogen's expression telegraphed that she was both intrigued and surprised. "What is it with you and Pierre?"

"I don't know what you're talking about," said Ophelia, getting up to clear her plate from the table and placing it in the sink.

"Yes, you do! That sort of ease of familiarity that says you've been in each other's company a great deal when apparently you haven't. And that undertone of attraction—" She stopped short. "Were you sweethearts?"

Ophelia's shoulders began to shake, robbing her of speech.

Imogen narrowed her eyes. "There is something you're hiding from me."

"Well, it isn't that!" declared Ophelia when she had regained control of her senses. She blew her nose and wiped her ivory cheeks.

Imogen pointed a finger. "So, there *is* something. And why this resistance to suspecting him?"

Ophelia shrugged. "His suave and gallant manner, I suppose. Not to mention he *is* unusually handsome." Her eyes lost their focus and Imogen wondered if her sister was interested in a romantic relationship with Pierre.

There was still time.

Pierre's Antiques Emporium was nestled close to the end of the high street, flanked by similar black and white shops. Pierre was a master at window display and even though the high, small, Elizabethan windows gave limited space, he managed to create scenes that looked like someone had just been called to the telephone. Shimmering gold satin displayed period jewels and mother of pearl encrusted hairbrushes from centuries before, in such a way that you wanted to go right in and snap up the treasure before someone else beat you to it. Even their thrifty mother had fallen prey to Pierre's talents.

Ophelia pushed on the door and they were engulfed in aged wood, with faint hints of furniture polish and Pierre's signature sandalwood cologne. Rich wooden shelves lined the far walls, displaying an array of vintage clocks, ornate vases and aging books. Though both twins felt the magnetism of the books, they were here for bigger items today.

Not an inch of space was wasted in this Aladdin's treasure trove. Every nook and cranny housed unique pieces meticulously arranged with art and style; porcelain figurines, pictures with gilded frames, Victorian curios and even some medieval artifacts. The familiar feel of immersion in the past, swept over the pair.

"Bonjour! Bonjour!" Pierre emerged flicking a lavender silk kerchief and wiping his neatly trimmed white mustache. He pushed it into the pocket of his masterfully tailored, paisley waistcoat. "Apologies! I was indulging in a little 'elevenses'. One of my favorite English meals."

He leaned forward to kiss each sister on the cheeks. Ophelia unabashedly drank in his aura.

"I remember you telling me you're interested in new furniture," he began. "As I mentioned, I 'ave recently received delivery of some curated items from a certain distressed duchess from Yorkshire who shall remain anonymous. If you will please follow me, they are in the storage area in the back. I did not want to display them without giving you first refusal."

"So kind of you," said Imogen, weaving through the trinkets in the main store as she followed in his wake. Given his age, Pierre was very quick on his feet.

They passed through his office where a Georgian clock lay disemboweled on his desk beneath a high-powered magnifying glass on a stand. Above it, a light shone down.

Pierre's particular expertise was in restoring antique clocks. His reputation for this ability was nationwide.

They passed into a confined yard and Pierre opened the door to a more modern shed-like structure. He flicked on a row of electric lights that revealed a jumble of chairs, sofas, chaises and bedframes. On the periphery were chests of drawers, tallboys and dressing tables.

"I can attest to the high quality of every item in this batch." He winked. "Everything here has my seal of approval. Can I interest you in this reclining couch?"

He drew their attention to a cherry wood chaise with beautiful curves, the seat covered in a thick, mint taffeta. Ophelia could imagine herself reclining upon it with a cup of tea.

"Oh, yes!" said Ophelia at the same time Imogen cried, "Oh, no!"

Pierre's mustache wiggled. "I see we are not quite in agreement."

"It won't do for the sitting room, of course, but it will be lovely by the window in my bedroom." Ophelia turned to Imogen. "I shall only have one bed in there. Plenty of room. Then I can redecorate in tones that match the chaise."

"If you say so." Imogen looked over the other furniture. "Can you show me that one?" She pointed to a sturdy but comfortable looking, deep orange, damask sofa.

Pierre removed his monocle and shifted a dining chair and an occasional table to let Imogen examine the couch. "Try it out."

She sank into a down stuffed, padded seat. "Oh, this is lovely. Try it, Ophelia."

"Very nap worthy," agreed her sister.

After an hour of picking out new furniture for the sitting room and bedrooms and negotiating prices, Imogen asked, "What do you suggest we do with our old stuff? It's rather ancient and not in the best condition."

"Not a problem," replied Pierre. "I know an orphanage that will be more than grateful for such solid pieces. When my delivery men bring your new furniture, they can remove your existing items and take them straight there. The couple that run it are old friends and were bemoaning the state of their current furnishings."

"Perfect!" proclaimed Ophelia.

Pierre took them back to the main store. "'Ow are you settling in?"

"It's like coming home," she replied.

"Which it is," added Imogen. "What was it like for you when you first arrived in Saffron Weald, Pierre? Villages are notoriously bad at accepting new people." She flashed a mischievous grin in his direction. "Especially foreigners."

A slight tip of the head and a drag on his bottom lip betrayed that the memory was not all pleasant. "That is true. The first year was difficult, I will admit, but when people appreciated the quality of products I provided and the strength of my expertise, I won them over. They now take great pride in my reputation as an 'orologist of the first order." He blew a chef's kiss with his fingers.

"What year would that have been?" asked Imogen, fingering a heavy silver locket displayed on a stand.

"1900. We knew nothing of war then." Imogen thought he glanced at Ophelia. "They were
'appy times."

"Why did you move from your home in France? La Vendée wasn't it?" asked Ophelia.

"You 'ave a good memory, ma chérie. Yes. The west coast, below Brittany. Work really. I 'ad apprenticed with an antique dealer and 'e sent me to London to look over an estate. I was enamored. I settled my affairs in France, came with only the clothes on my back, as the saying goes, and came to seek my fortune."

"When was that?" asked Imogen.

"1885. I was barely twenty-three. It was the perfect time."

"Most people are married by then. You had no one?" asked Imogen, hoping he would not find the question too personal.

A shadow passed over his dark eyes. "I 'ad a sweetheart, but she died from the fever before we could marry. My grief was as a bottomless pit of despair, but when I emerged, I found the memories surrounding me constrictive. Moving to London was the perfect tonic."

"Oh, Pierre! So sad! And you never found anyone else?" she exclaimed.

"No one could replace Geneviève in my heart." He patted the left pocket of his waistcoat. "I keep her memory locked in my 'eart. I believe that one day we will be together again."

"Pierre, that is so romantic," murmured Imogen as if speaking aloud would break some kind of spell.

"Romantic? Yes. But lonely." He glanced at Ophelia who did not look away and Imogen had the feeling of being a gooseberry once again.

He rubbed his hands. "Now, when will you delight us with your playing?" he asked Ophelia.

"I think once we've got our new furniture in and repainted everything. Before that I shan't have time to really practice."

"Then I shall hold you to it. I love to hear your music."
Imogen frowned. "You've heard Ophelia play?"
Ophelia's head snapped up.

"Ah, yes," he said stiffly. "I 'ad the pleasure of going to 'ear her orchestra whenever I was in London." Imogen glanced from her sister to Pierre. "Your mother recommended I go," he finished.

"Have you heard any more about the murdered girl?" asked Ophelia, clasping her handbag with both hands.

Pierre's shoulders relaxed. "No. You?"

"You know she was not who she said she was?" Ophelia asked.

"I did 'ear that much, yes. What was she doing 'ere?" Imogen caught Ophelia's eye.

"It seems like she was making an investigation of some sort into the people in the village."

A subtle change in the tension revealed his interest. "Whatever for?"

"Not sure." Imogen prevaricated. "But if she was using an assumed name, she must have thought it too dangerous to use her own, don't you think?"

"I suppose so," murmured Pierre, his brow furrowed slightly.

"Did you meet her?" asked Ophelia.

"The dead girl? As a member of the organizing committee, she 'ad wanted to speak to all of us, but she never made it to me before…well, you know." He ran a finger along his trim mustache. "Did you?"

"Oh, yes," replied Ophelia. "She interviewed us for her paper—but of course that was just a ruse. She was very interested when she discovered we had grown up in the village and had now returned."

"I expect so," he mumbled, but his thoughts were clearly elsewhere. "Terrible thing. Do they even know who she really was?"

Ophelia made a unilateral decision which earned a pinched look from her sister. "We heard from the colonel that her real name was Willa Medford."

Pierre's eyes were unreadable as he tipped his head and considered. "Doesn't mean anything to me, I'm afraid."

"So young," murmured Imogen. "It's always worse when the victim is in their youth with their whole life ahead of them."

"Are you in the 'abit of finding dead bodies?" he asked, the twinkle back in his eye.

# Chapter 15

"So, Pierre was here during the important time frame," pointed out Imogen as they stepped out of his store. "Lovely though he may be, he *must* stay on the list."

Ophelia gritted her teeth. "If you say so, ducky."

"I do. Police work is nothing if not methodical. If Pierre is innocent, the facts will bear it out." She withdrew a small shopping list from her bag. "Now, let's get our bread, and have a little chat with the Puddingfields."

There was a queue of people in the bakery. The Puddingfields had cleverly placed a fan in one of the small windowpanes that pushed the heavenly smell of baking bread out onto the street. Like Pavlov's dog experiment, it worked like a charm.

The colonel was in line ahead of them and doffed his hat.

"Did you have a fun day in London, Colonel?" Imogen asked.

Only the most attentive would have noticed the trace of confusion that flickered through his brows. "Excuse me?"

"Oh, we went gallivanting yesterday and saw you at the train station on the platform for London."

He recovered. "Oh, yes. Yes. Actually, I got off in Kingston. Seeing an old colleague for the day."

Imogen was not one hundred percent sure he was telling the truth. But why not?"

"Where did *you* go?" He squinted a smile.

Now it was their turn to be evasive. "We felt in need of a little escape and took a short excursion into the countryside," she replied.

"I know what you mean," he confided. "This blasted murder business is like a pall over the whole village. Hope the police figure out who the culprit is soon. Need to get back to normal. Makes the ladies hysterical." He lowered his voice. "Connie got a ruddy great beast of a dog for protection. Looks like it would take your hand off. Personally, I think it's too big for her to handle."

"She mentioned her intention of doing that during the coffee hour after church. But I didn't think she'd actually do it," said Ophelia in disbelief.

"Funny. She didn't mention the dog when we were at the library," mused Imogen.

"So, you've started researching for the history, then?" the colonel asked as they inched closer to the counter.

"Yes, and we found a mention of you, Colonel."

His face lit up. "Me?"

"It was in a volume on people of note from the county. It detailed your battlefield promotion in the Second Boar War."

A pink hue suffused the colonel's face. "Did it indeed? Anyone would have done the same." He seemed humbly embarrassed by the mention, which description did not always come to mind when thinking of the colonel.

The queue moved forward again.

"Did you visit Saffron Weald much when you were married?" Ophelia asked.

The colonel's lips twisted. "Rather a strained relationship with my father. Only came for birthdays and the occasional Christmas. Visited much more when it was just Mother."

Ophelia recalled the slight woman with a puff of blonde hair that later turned snow white. Even as a young woman, she had flinched easily and blinked excessively, and though Mrs. Winstanley had never been called robust, she definitely evolved into a more confident version of herself once her bully of a husband died.

"You?" he asked.

"I came as often as my schedule allowed. I performed a lot over Christmas so that was not the best time for me.

And then Mother would come to see some of my performances."

"We would have Mother for the holidays when the children were young," added Imogen. "Much easier moving one person than the four of us and all the gifts. Our house was plenty big enough and we kept a room for her. But like Ophelia, we visited as often as we could. My children adored her."

"Yes. Fine woman, your mother. Stiff backbone." He gave a half shake of the head. "Good friend to my mother when she was alive."

"Yes, Mother was very sensitive to the needs of others," agreed Ophelia. "Went out of her way to make sure everyone was included. Quite the legacy."

The queue moved once more and Imogen could see that they were going to lose their window of opportunity.

"What year did your father die?" she asked.

The colonel screwed up his eyes. "1895. Summer. Stroke."

"Ahh." Imogen nodded. *The colonel began more regular visits before 1908.*

"And your mother?" asked Ophelia.

"1913. Right before the Great War. Glad she didn't live to see it, frankly."

"When did you move back to the village?"

"After my wife, Margaret, died. That was 1910."

Ophelia knew that the colonel and his wife had not been blessed with children.

"Colonel," said Arthur Puddingfield, putting an end to their inquiries. "What can I get for you today?"

The colonel bowed to the sisters and turned to the counter to place his order.

The twins made faces at each other behind his back. The colonel was certainly still in the running, as he had been a visitor to the village in the correct time frame. He would have to stay on the list. And Imogen still was not quite sure she believed his tale about going to Kingston. Plus, Willa had interviewed him. What if she had actually confronted him about killing her mother and he had bopped her on the head? Imogen's heart felt heavy. Murder made one *so* suspicious.

The colonel spun around with a country cob wrapped in grease paper. "Good day, ladies."

Mr. Puddingfield rubbed his hands as he looked over their shoulders at the string of people still waiting. "What can I get you, ladies?"

Considering the size of the crowd, it was not a convenient time to ask pointed questions so they ordered a loaf and some doughnuts. As he wrapped them, he asked, "Alice and I were talking. We'd love to have you over for dinner. Would tomorrow night at seven work?"

"Splendid. Looking forward to it," replied Ophelia.

Back out on the street, they ran straight into Mildred who was not looking where she was going. The crusty, round loaf wobbled out of Imogen's grasp. Ophelia saved the bread rugby fashion and bundled it into her shopping basket.

"A thousand apologies," gasped Mildred. "I'm a bit flustered and wasn't paying attention." She straightened her hideous, brown hat, looking into the bakers with a deep frown. "Think I'll finish up my other errands first." She slapped her forehead. "But bumping into you will save me one. I was planning on coming over to the cottage to tell you about the Women's Institute meeting tomorrow. We're throwing a little party to welcome you both home."

Ophelia's heart went through a kaleidoscope of emotions. Gratefulness that they did not have to entertain Mildred at home since she had a reputation as harder to get rid of than a raspberry stain, and dread that they were being summoned to the W.I.

Imogen caught her sister's eye. "How nice of you. Of course, we'll be there. Can we bring anything? And what time?"

"Three o'clock," Mildred answered. "As the honored guests you need bring nothing." She hurried on but called over her shoulder. "See you tomorrow."

"Our social calendar is filling up," chuckled Ophelia. "At least it will give us the occasion to ask our questions in a natural setting."

A shadow passed over the high street and they both looked up. "Time to hurry home."

# Chapter 16

An oval metal plaque on the wall of the village hall declared that the Women's Institute of Saffron Weald had been established in 1805. Its original mission had been to help with the funerals of those in the village who died. Whether or not that was still a function of the organization, Ophelia did not know, but what she did know was that its current charter was far broader some one hundred years later. The W.I. had its fingers in many village pies. Some might say, too many pies.

Unlike the ornate church with its fenestrations, arched bell tower and embattled parapet, the village hall was severely utilitarian in design. A basic stage stood at one end and scuffed parquet covered the floor.

Someone had gone to the effort of placing small jars of bright flowers on the white tablecloths. Tiered plates carried all sorts of delicate cakes and a silver tea urn stood on a table along a wall.

Seven women stood as the twins entered with a little ripple of applause and Imogen wondered if all newcomers received the same ovation or if this was because their mother had been an integral part of the association and that this was really a posthumous show of appreciation to honor her.

Mildred stepped forward wearing a gaudy red hat supporting another stuffed bird, and a sash pronouncing her the president of the organization.

"Welcome! Please, sit here at the top of the table with me."

Ophelia and Imogen acknowledged Connie, Prudence Cresswell, the vicar's wife, Rosalind Bloomfield, the florist, Harriet Cleaver, the butcher's wife, Patricia Snodgrass, the postmistress, and Agatha Trumble, headmistress of the little school. The sweetshop owner was glaringly absent—she was far too new to the village to warrant a spot.

"Well, isn't this nice?" began Mildred. "In a reversal of our usual agenda, we will visit first and discuss business second. All in favor?"

Everyone raised their hands and Imogen wasn't sure what to do with hers.

"That's settled then. Connie, I'll put you in charge of the tea, if you don't mind?"

Connie scraped back her chair with a scowl and Mildred began a breathless recounting of the W.I.'s recent history. Ophelia suppressed a sigh.

"Feel at home yet?" asked the vicar's wife, when Mildred took a deeper breath. Prudence Cresswell reminded Imogen of a stick of celery, tall and thin with a riot of uncontrollable curly hair.

"Badger's Hollow has always felt like home," replied Imogen. "We just want to put our own stamp on it."

"Oh?"

"Yes, we've just purchased a whole stack of new furniture from Pierre and are going to paint—well, we're not actually going to paint, we're going to hire someone to do it, throughout. Then we will pick out some new rugs."

"Oh, Pierre!" sighed the vicar's wife as though she were speaking of a movie star from Hollywood. "What a charming man. And such exquisite taste. I tell all my friends about his talent with clocks." She suddenly seemed to remember she was married and cleared her throat. "Your mother liked the cottage the way it was but I see no problem with changing it now."

"That was our opinion," said Ophelia. "Make it our own. Though Mother's essence is still in the very air we breathe and every particle of the house."

"I don't doubt it," said Prudence. "I used to love to pass her cottage and hear the opera pouring from the open windows. I'll confess, I'd sometimes stop to see if I could spot her dancing around. She didn't care what anyone thought. It was refreshing."

That much was true. Beatrice Harrington was truly one of a kind. Spontaneous, impetuous and passionate about her causes. Ophelia was more like her. Imogen took after their steady, measured father who watched his wife's antics with a fatherly smile. Beatrice Harrington dared to do what he only dreamed of doing.

"Yes. Mother made our childhood magical," said Imogen. "No ant was too insignificant, no spider too hairy for a nature lesson. We miss her terribly. That's why living in her home is so healing."

Mildred's head bobbed like a pigeon as she tried to infiltrate the conversation but fortunately someone called to her from the other end of the table. She stood to move.

"It must be full of rich memories sparked by the sights and smells of the place," the vicar's wife agreed.

"You've hit the nail on the head," Ophelia affirmed.

"Do you have plans other than redecorating?"

Ophelia caught Imogen's eye. "We do in fact," said Ophelia. "We've learned that Mother began writing a history of Saffron Weald. We've decided to finish what she started. It's a project we hope will keep our minds sharp."

"Did you find her notes?" asked Prudence.

Imogen gave a slight tip of the head to indicate that she would lead the way forward. "Well, Mother had mentioned the project in passing, but then her time came. We haven't found any of her documentation, so we weren't sure if she had actually started." It was a fine tapestry of truth and fiction.

"I don't think it was common knowledge," admitted the vicar's wife. "I happened to see her tucked in a corner of the library with a stack of history texts one day, and asked if she was researching her family history. I have an interest in heraldry myself."

The twins leaned forward as one.

"I surprised her," continued Prudence, "and she blurted out that she had ideas of writing a history as a legacy and would I keep it under my hat as she had no confidence in her skills as a writer."

"Did you happen to see the book she kept her notes in?" asked Imogen.

"Well, if it was the one she had with her that day, it was leather with a gold crest on the front and gold colored spirals holding the pages together."

A desire to do the subject to death in private with her sister, grabbed hold of Ophelia and she had to drink a gulp of tea to dilute the impulse. First the colonel and now the vicar's wife was telling them that their mother was really writing a history of the village. The truth was that their mother had never mentioned anything of the sort to them. In fact, they knew for certain that their mother hated writing. She found the physical and mental process draining and much preferred expressing herself through music. *What was she really doing?* Ophelia glanced up to see a similar hankering, pulsing through her sister's gray blue eyes. She knew instinctively that they both wanted to leave immediately and tear the house apart. However, only the slight flare of Imogen's nose betrayed the mental wrestle in which she was engaged.

"I don't know much about you, Mrs. Cresswell," said Ophelia. "Where are your people from?" Since they were stuck here as honored guests, they might as well exploit the moment to gather intelligence.

"Redhill. Surrey. Cresswell came to our parish as a curate and well…" her greenish skin blushed orange. "We fell in love."

"Where is the reverend from again?" asked Ophelia, though she knew perfectly well.

"Arbor Langley in Wiltshire. He attended divinity school at Cambridge and then secured the post of curate in

Redhill. We had never been to Hampshire before coming here. Saffron Weald is a hidden jewel."

"So, neither of you had family or friends here? That was very brave," commented Imogen.

Prudence Cresswell's head twitched. "Those in the Lord's service are sometimes called upon to put others before self. It comes with the job. But we do love it here." She raised her shoulders. "In fact, I hope we never have to leave."

Connie returned from filling all the cups and sat on the other side of the table. Her brow was clouded. "I don't see why *I* have to do all the teas," she murmured.

"Did we hear you got a dog?" asked Imogen to try and chase the clouds of discontent away.

Connie's mood dipped farther. "Flipping great monster! I had half a mind not to come to this for fear he would tear my little house to shreds. Do you know, while I was at work yesterday, the rascal took one of my cushions and ripped it to pieces? Feathers everywhere! And my poor kitty, Marmaduke, is a bag of nerves. Won't come out from under my bed." She drummed nervous fingers on the table. "To be honest, I don't know if I can keep him."

"Perhaps a spaniel would be better?" suggested the vicar's wife. "We love our Lucy. She's so calm and obedient."

Connie shook her head, salt and pepper curls swaying. "No. I need a guard dog. I've no husband to keep me safe."

"How about a Labrador?" suggested Imogen. "We had one for years—not for hunting you understand—and Wilfred loved that dog. Me too. He was gentle but would become protective when circumstances warranted."

"Where did you get your dog?" asked Ophelia.

"Farmer Tidwell found him as a stray several years ago. I mentioned that I was looking for a guard dog and he suggested I give Tiny a try. Talk about a misnomer. Tiny's used to living outdoors in wide open spaces, not cooped up in a little cottage. And he takes *me* for a walk. I think he's done my back in."

"Would the farmer take him back?" asked Ophelia. "Just tell him the dog isn't working out."

"I hate to do that before I find a replacement," Connie said, biting her nails. "With a murderer around I feel completely vulnerable."

"There's an RSPCA in Lounsdon. You could see if they have any Labradors," said Prudence.

Connie puffed air through her hair. "I might have to do that. I can't live like this."

Mildred returned and tapped a spoon against her cup. "Ladies! Time for our meeting to begin. First agenda item, the flowers at the bottom of the war memorial."

# Chapter 17

The W.I. agenda was interminable. Ophelia came up with a dozen crazy scenarios that would allow them to leave early but a warning look from Imogen prevented her. However, eventually, the meeting ended, and the twins made their escape.

Immediately they were out of earshot, the sisters began to chatter about the fact that unbeknownst to them, their mother had begun a history of Saffron Weald.

"I thought it was just idle chatter when the colonel told us about it, and the suggestion gave us a good reason to begin digging into the life of the village, but now it seems that Mother was doing exactly what *we* are claiming to do," cried Ophelia." "It's kismet!"

"Seems fishy to me. She hated any kind of study and writing," pointed out Imogen.

"I know. What could she have been up to?"

Almost skipping home, they blasted through the white gate, nearly colliding in their haste to get through the front door. Within minutes, they were headfirst in various cupboards and drawers trying to unearth the little leather notebook.

After two solid hours of searching and ingesting more dust than was healthy in women of their age, clutching strained back muscles, they hobbled over to reconnect at the kitchen table.

"Nothing! Perhaps she had it buried with her," suggested Ophelia.

Imogen giggled. "I hardly think so, lovey."

"But where can it be? We've searched everywhere I can think of."

"I don't know," conceded Imogen. "But I think it's time for another cup of tea. I'm parched. We haven't even found Mother's recipe book."

"This cottage is very good at keeping its secrets," declared Ophelia.

Imogen rose to fill the big kettle in the sink. Carrying it back to the stove she accidentally dropped the lid down the side as she tried to replace it.

"*Oh, nutmegs!*" She bent down to retrieve the lid but the round knob had popped off and rolled into the narrow, dark space between the wall and the stove.

"Hand me a fire poker," she demanded.

Ophelia pushed up her weary bones, grabbed the poker and handed it to her sister. Imogen thrust it between the wall and the oven.

"It's so dark back here," Imogen complained. "See if there's a torch, lovey."

"Now, where did I just see one?" murmured Ophelia as she retraced her steps. "Here it is! On the top shelf of the larder." She pressed the button but it did not ignite. Wiggling it finally produced a dim beam. "Here."

Without turning around, Imogen reached her arm back and grabbed the torch, shining it into the abyss. "Oh, I see it!" she said. "Come and hold the light high while I poke."

Bottom up, Imogen jabbed, prodded and pulled. After several minutes she cried, "Voilà!" and the little round handle rolled out. "Wait!" She stabbed around some more then dragged the poker back, lifting a treasure in the air. "Mother's recipe book! It must have fallen down the side when she was cooking." As Imogen held it aloft, something dropped out.

A gold spiraled leather notebook.

Tea forgotten, the sisters took their mother's book to the table, sitting side by side.

"I'm almost afraid to look," said Imogen.

"Why?" asked Ophelia.

"I don't know. I have a funny feeling."

"Here. Let me do it then," said Ophelia.

They opened the cover and saw their mother's familiar chicken scratch.

*Notes.*

"Well, that's anti-climactic," said Ophelia with a wry smile.

She turned the page.

*NJMESFE DIVNGPSE*

*Mbssjfe*

*Cpso jo uif wjmmbhf. Mfgu gps b gfx zfbst cvu sfuvsofe up ublf pg xjepxfe npuifs jo 21014.*

"What in the world," cried Imogen as Ophelia flicked through the pages and pages of gobbledygook.

"It's a code," said Ophelia with authority.

"How do you know that?" demanded Imogen.

"*The Times* crosswords and puzzles," she responded, without missing a beat. "Now which one mother used, I don't know. Get me some paper, will you."

Imogen found some scrap paper in a drawer and a stubby pencil.

"Let's try the letter after these letters in the alphabet." Ophelia wrote, OKNFTGF. "No, that's nonsense. Now I'll try the preceding letter." She wrote, MILDRED.

The sisters locked eyes.

"That's it!"

Ophelia transcribed the first page using the simple code.

*Unmarried. Born in the village. Left for a few years but returned to take care of her widowed mother in 1903.*

"This looks eerily familiar," gasped Imogen, hand to her mouth. "And not at all like notes for a history of the village. Do you think Mother was helping Willa by looking into the lives of the people in the village like we are?"

Ophelia turned another page and transcribed.

*REVEREND BARTHOLOMEW CRESSWELL*

*Grew up in the village next to Willa. Coincidence? Born 1886. Moved to Saffron Weald 1920. Had a friend who lived in a village nearby when he was a boy. Related?*

"That contradicts what his wife said," Imogen pointed out. "Wonder who it is?"

Ophelia ploughed on with the transcription.

REGINALD TUMBLETHORN

*Born 1885. Never moved. Never married. Eccentric. Wounded early in the war. Didn't react when I mentioned West Wallop. Was living here in 1908.*

"It seems as though she was going through the inhabitants just as we are but died before she discovered anything of real worth," said Ophelia. "It's fate willing us to carry on her work."

"Well, let's keep going," said Imogen, her cheeks flushed.

ARTHUR PUDDINGFIELD

*Brother of Ophelia's first love.*

"Sentimental mush," choked Ophelia. "We weren't at all compatible!"

*What was Arthur doing behind the public house Saturday last, around midnight? Are he and the Missus as happy as they portray after the death of their son. Here in 1908.*

"What on earth was mother doing up at midnight on a Saturday?" asked Imogen.

Ophelia pointed at the date. "June 23. Midsummer's Eve. You know mother and her pagan leanings. I bet she was frolicking with the fairies."

"True. Who's next?"

Ophelia turned the page.

PIERRE ANCIEN

*Charming man of mystery. Why choose Saffron Weald? Are all his travels to find antique treasures or is there a clandestine nature to some of them?*

"Do you think Mother was losing her marbles?" asked Imogen.

"Mother was as sane as you or I. Well, me anyway." She gave her sister a friendly shove.

They went back to the notebook.

*Why did he not marry? He would disappear for weeks during the war. Why? Where did he go? Here in 1908. Where was he in 1907?*

CONNIE FEATHERSTONE

*Born shortly after the twins. Lived with parents and grandparents. Didn't the family used to live in a larger home before she was born? Check 1861 census.*

"That's news to me," said Ophelia. "Do you recall any of that?"

Imogen pulled her mouth down. "No. I can only remember them being at the cottage."

"Do you recall what Connie said about her uncle losing the family money, though. Could be true."

COLONEL WINSTANLEY

*Born here but married and moved away. Came back in 1903 after his wife died and his father. Did he know Willa's mother? Did they ever meet? Has he been to Wiltshire? Why does he not like to talk about his time in the Boer War?*

"She seems to be asking the same questions—"
*Woosh!*

The back door suddenly swished open and in one swift movement Ophelia brushed her arm across the table letting the notebook drop into her lap.

"Connie!" said Imogen. "How lovely!"

Hadn't they just seen her at the W.I. meeting? What was she doing here?

"Now that you're settled in, we can be backdoor friends, like everyone else." Her eyes beamed with expectation.

"Even with a murderer running around?—your words, Connie."

"Oh, yes! I suppose you're right. Did I give you a shock?"

"You did rather. We were in the middle of something."

"Ooh! What was it?" Connie moved toward the table.

The sisters made eye contact.

"We found mother's recipe book," said Ophelia, quickly.

"Oh?" There was a measure of disappointment bound up in Connie's exclamation.

"Well, we were having a Dicken's of a time finding it, so the book's discovery is more exciting for us than you. Some of Mother's recipes are legend."

"Oh, I know," said Connie. "No one's coffee cake could match Bea's. Not even the Puddingfield's. I just thought maybe you'd found an old family heirloom by the wonder in your eyes. One that you'd take to Pierre and discover was worth thousands of pounds." She flapped her hands. "Or, or a key to a mysterious lock that would uncover a stash of Spanish gold."

"Connie, I think you've been reading too many books, ducky," said Ophelia.

"That's as maybe," she agreed. "I certainly prefer fictional worlds."

"Well, *we* are very happy the recipe book has been found as we promised the vicar we'd make him some coffee cake when we came upon it."

"Right." Connie stared blankly into space.

"Did you come here for a reason, lovey, or just to pass the time of day?" asked Imogen.

"Oh, yes. Mildred forgot to present you both with the W.I. pins. So unlike her. I don't know what's the matter with her. Anyway, I said I'd drop them along." She reached into her cream, leather handbag and withdrew two round pins, her eyes full of expectation.

"How lovely," murmured Imogen, feeling that the pins were an assumption that they were going full throttle into the W.I. which they had not decided on at all.

Connie looked at her watch. "Time to go and get ready for bell ringing practice. Are either of you going to join us?"

"Imogen has an arthritic shoulder and I haven't had a chance to consider it yet, Connie. Give me some time."

The librarian's shoulders rose a smidgen as her lips turned down. "No matter. I'm still working on Pierre. He would make going to practice a real treat." Then she giggled like a sixteen-year-old girl and left as fast as she had come.

Imogen watched Connie through the kitchen window as she walked out the kitchen door and around the back of the house. "She's gone!"

Ophelia pulled up the notebook and flipped it open again, scribbling the real words from the code.

"Oh!"

Imogen watched as her sister's face collapsed. Speechless, she pointed to the writing on the page.

Imogen's eyes found the words.

*I think someone has connected my so-called research to the disappearance of Willa's mother. I can sense someone watching me.*

*If you are reading this, I have been murdered.*

# Chapter 18

Imogen's blood ran cold. "Murdered? But Mother was ninety-five. It was just her time. That's what the doctor said. I-I think she was being overly dramatic."

"Do you?" asked Ophelia, brows raised. "Willa approaches our mother in a letter asking about her own mother's disappearance. Mother remembers Mrs. Medford and decides to help the young girl. She begins a clandestine investigation but is not experienced in such things and knowing Mother, was not as inconspicuous as she thought she was. Then she dies. No one questioned her passing because she was so old."

Imogen's throat filled with fear. "You really think someone bumped her off?"

"Look, I don't know for certain but one minute she's making, what she thinks are discreet inquiries—and we both know mother wasn't subtle at the best of times—and the next she dies in her sleep. I think given this message from her own hand, it's a distinct possibility."

Imogen could feel her eyes pricking. "Kill Mother? It's unconscionable."

"Let's look at the facts we know," said Ophelia. "A man is pushed down a well in 1907. Willa's mother, Mrs. Medford, has reason to believe it is foul play and can't scratch the itch of suspicion away. She recalls a stranger in the village around the time of the gentleman's disappearance and somehow knows they have a connection to Saffron Weald."

"Perhaps she spoke to them?" suggested Imogen. "Or they asked for directions."

"That could well be. Anyway, Willa's mother decides to come to Saffron Weald in pursuit of the person she saw a year before, the person she thinks might be responsible, and is struck on the head with a rock. I know the police report said she fell and hit her head, but I don't believe it for a minute.

"Twenty years later, her daughter discovers that her mother did not die of natural causes as she was told, and that she talked to *our* mother, Beatrice Harrington, while visiting the village. Willa writes to her, and Mother's response seems promising. She writes again but this time receives no answer. So, Willa comes to Saffron Weald incognito and is coshed on the head."

"Three murders," murmured Imogen, hand to her neck.

"Four, if you count Mother."

Imogen's hands were clammy. "And you think they were all committed by the same person?"

"It certainly looks that way."

A chill ran through Imogen and she shivered, rubbing her arms. "Someone just walked over my grave."

Raising her palms, Ophelia warned, "Let's not panic, ducky. If we could have mother exhumed, the police can run a test to see if there is something like poison in her system. Then we would know for sure."

Imogen jerked. "What? Exhumed? Are you mad? This is Mother we're talking about."

Ophelia remained annoyingly calm. "It's the only way to know for sure."

All of a sudden, Imogen felt emotionally fragile. Putting a hand to her mouth, she moaned, "I can't bear the thought."

"How does one go about arranging such a thing?" Ophelia's mouth pulled down as her nails drummed the table. "Do we start with the local police?"

"They won't believe us!" cried Imogen. "It's not like we have proof."

"No, you're right. We need to solve Willa's murder first." Ophelia snapped her fingers. "But we *could* talk to the doctor who attended Mother about our suspicions."

Staring at her sister as if she were a stranger, Imogen attempted to process Ophelia's business-like attitude in the face of this catastrophic revelation about their mother's passing. This was not the response of a normal person. Imogen was beginning to wonder if she really knew her sister at all.

"I confess, I've lost my enthusiasm for the task," said Imogen in a small voice. "And if you're right, meddling might make us sitting ducks."

An impulsive zeal spread across Ophelia's lined features. "Mother and Willa were alone. *We* have each other. That should keep us safe. We'll just keep doing what we were doing, being careful not to poke the beehive."

Imogen quivered. Her peaceful retirement was crumbling before her eyes.

"Better put on a happy face, ducky. We're having dinner with the Puddingfields tonight," Ophelia reminded her.

"No! Oh, I can't go, Ophelia! Unlike you, I'm too upset," she blustered, shoulders slumping.

Ophelia arched a brow. "I'm shaken by it all too, Imogen, but this information has set a fire under me to get to the bottom of the matter. I still feel some responsibility to delve into Willa's murder." She slapped the table. "But we absolutely cannot let someone get away with taking Mother's life."

"Well, when you put it like that...but I've no appetite and I'm a terrible liar. The Puddingfields will be able to tell there's something wrong, immediately." She thrust up her head, alarm etched into every feature. "Do you think Mother suffered? Was she scared?"

"Imogen, you need to calm yourself. That is something we cannot know. What we do know is that Mother died in her sleep and is now at peace after a long and happy life. We need to focus on that. It will do no good to whip ourselves into hysteria."

The Puddingfield's two story cottage looked like it had been built by a drunken sailor. On the other side of the village, it sat on the edge of an acre of land that had been left to its own devices. The reddish tile roof dipped low over the upper windows and contrasted with the crisp white of the walls and black timbers. A hand-styled fence of woven branches surrounded the property.

It had taken Ophelia some time to persuade her sister that they should keep the appointment. With an aching heart, Imogen knocked on the arched timber door that had been bought at an auction from a derelict fourteenth century abbey in Yorkshire. Wrought iron curlicues decorated the wood.

"Welcome," said Archie, his smile spreading across his whole face. Ophelia offered their bottle of wine.

"You shouldn't have."

The ceiling of the hall was so low that everyone had to duck as they followed the mouthwatering smell of beef bourguignon. A wall had been knocked down to make the kitchen big enough for the bakers' tastes. Alice was at a large oven stirring something that smelled divine. In spite of the dread that had taken up permanent residence in her chest, Imogen's mouth watered.

"Ophelia! Imogen!" cried Alice in welcome, then she tutted. "Archie, you should have taken them to the lounge not the kitchen!"

"Nonsense! We don't need to stand on ceremony with them. They're backdoor friends," he responded.

Imogen thought of the same phrase Connie had used that afternoon after barging in. Was it a 'back door friend' who had killed their mother? She swept the errant thought away.

"We don't mind at all," agreed Ophelia. "What is that you're cooking?"

Alice wiped her cheek that had none of the droop most people experienced at her age. "It's a sauce for the dessert. Just a little thing I picked up from a French chef in Brighton, years ago."

"Well, it smells divine."

"Thank you. Can we get you a drink? Sherry?" Alice asked.

"Perhaps a little," said Ophelia.

"Me too," added Imogen, hoping the strong wine would help settle her nerves.

Archie disappeared out the door and Alice gestured for them to sit down at the ebony brown table.

"Pierre found this table for us. Much bigger than a usual kitchen piece. Suits us down to the ground." Her hair was in a flattering chignon that showed off her long neck.

"I'm surprised you like to cook at home since you do it all day at the shop," remarked Ophelia.

"Oh, we rarely do," Alice said with a smile. "But we go all out when friends are coming over."

Archie returned with several small glasses on a silver tray. He handed them round.

"Cheers!" he said, lifting the glass.

"Cheers!" they all responded. Imogen tried hard to act as though her whole world had not just fallen apart.

"How was the W.I?" Alice asked. "I begged off saying I had too much to bake, but that's not entirely true. I know they mean well, but…" She let the sentence trail off.

"We're feeling a bit steamrolled, if you must know," said Imogen, the strengthening warmth of the sherry hitting her veins. "They seem to assume that since Mother was so involved that it's automatic we'll join. We're still trying to adjust, if you must know. We've had a lot of change in a short timeframe, and what with the complication of the murder, we feel rather unsettled." *And you don't know the half of it!*

"Mmm," murmured Archie. "Never had a murder in Saffron Weald before. What is the world coming to?"

"Actually, that's not entirely true," corrected Ophelia.

Imogen blazed alarmed eyes at her sister. This comment was not her definition of discreet, confirmed by the charge that entered the room. Both Puddingfields put down their glasses.

"I beg your pardon?" said Alice.

Ophelia tried to chuckle to lighten the suddenly dark mood. "Yes, it's funny, really. We've started research for our little book and in a volume that contains a record of the colonel's medal, we found a reference to a murder that happened in 1909."

"It was 1908, lovey," corrected Imogen, trying to keep the anger out of her tone.

The bakers locked eyes.

"Well, that would mean…twenty years ago. I don't remember it," finished Archie.

"Me neither," said his wife. "You'd think it would have been big news."

"Well, it wasn't classified as a murder at the time. The official verdict was death by misadventure of an unidentified woman," explained Ophelia. "And the body was on Stirling land so maybe, since no one identified her and the body was found months after she died, it got buried, so to speak." She took a sip of the sherry and Imogen stiffened. "We've heard that this Lila, or Willa, thought she was the daughter of the unidentified woman."

Alice tensed. "Who told you that?"

"Uh, the colonel mentioned that the police found a notebook among her possessions and it was mentioned in there. She was trying to put all the pieces together."

"That would explain why she was here," said Archie.

"The death twenty years ago could still have been a tragic accident, as the police stated," said Alice, her brow furrowed.

"Then why kill the snooping girl?" asked Ophelia.

"My goodness!" declared Alice with a shudder. "You've given this some thought, haven't you?"

"A little, as we unpack," Ophelia admitted. "We bounce ideas off each other. It's rather nice for me to talk things over with someone. My plants never spoke back!"

Her joke succeeded in breaking the tension.

A scratching at the door meant the dog wanted to come in and the prickly conversation came to an end.

Relieved, Imogen scratched the terrier's ears.

"Let's go through into the dining room," said Alice. "My sauce is reducing nicely."

The room was long and narrow with a Henry VIII style banquet table. Heavy chairs ran the length of it.

"I thought we'd all sit together at the end," said Arthur showing the sisters to their seats.

Alice brought in a clear, light consommé soup and Archie opened their bottle of wine.

"To old friends," he toasted, lifting his glass.

"To old friends," everyone repeated.

"Tell me about your career in the symphony," said Alice. "Your mother spoke about it all the time."

For the next hour, Ophelia described the struggle to be respected as an all-female orchestra, the low pay and extensive travel involved.

"But you must have seen a great many parts of the continent," commented Alice.

"Oh, I did. We played in Florence, Nice, Paris, Brussels, and Amsterdam. That is until the stupid war."

"I should have liked to travel," Alice mused. "But bakers find it hard to take time off."

"I'm sure," said Ophelia. "Did you travel before your marriage?"

"Haha! No. Father was a tailor. Steady work but not particularly well paid. There were no extra funds for exotic holidays. Brighton was a great place to grow up, though.

The world came to us. Or at least Great Britain. I even saw the queen once."

"Was it hard for you to make a new home in tiny Saffron Weald?" asked Imogen.

"At first." Alice regarded her husband with soft eyes. "But I would have followed Archie to the ends of the earth."

Archie pressed his wife's hand and Ophelia felt the cold squeeze of loneliness in her heart. People thought she hadn't wanted to marry because she had a career, but that wasn't true. Like Alice, she would have given it all up for the right person.

"Did you travel, Archie? Apart from with the orchestra when we were young?" she asked.

"Not really. With Dad being a baker too, he had the same problem as us, you can't really take a holiday. Bread is best fresh. Then when he died young, I was expected to take over. That concert in Brighton was the furthest I'd ever been. Of course, we visited Alice's family when we could."

"Where do your children live now?" asked Imogen, indulging in the steamed pudding with Cointreau reduction.

"Peter lived with his wife in Wiltshire, near Holsworthy, before he died—" Archie shared a look of understanding with his wife and Imogen silently kicked herself as she remembered that their son had died in the war. "His wife went to live with her family, but she was good about bringing the grandchildren over when they were young. They're grown now. Peter was a chemist before the war. We were able to get him apprenticed when he showed little interest in bread."

"His son is engaged," added Alice. "And Rachel, she lives on a farm with her husband just fifteen miles away. She had three girls—kept trying for a boy but it never happened, bless her. Two are married and one still at home. Where do your children live, Imogen?"

"Fergus lives in London. He's a civil servant, and Penelope has a lovely home in Surrey, near Epsom Downs. She wanted me to go and live with her after Wilfred died but when Mother's will suggested Ophelia and I live together, I thought, why not? I'm not too old yet. There'll be plenty of time to live with my daughter when I find it hard to get around."

They spent the rest of the evening reminiscing about growing up in the village. The nostalgia and laughter helped the rock in Imogen's gut to soften.

Archie drove them home as it was dark and as soon as they walked in the door, Ophelia smiled like the Cheshire cat.

"Their son lived in Wiltshire!"

# Chapter 19

Imogen awoke to sun pouring through the open windows and bird song. Once fully awake, she lay in bed, focusing on her state of mind. Having marinated over night, the suggestion that their mother might not have passed away from natural causes, still left her feeling distinctly distressed. But something else was tugging at her brain. Another emotion.

Rolling onto her side, she recentered her thoughts directly on her mental malaise. In a flash of insight, she recognized that though she was still frightened, she was also angry. Furious. How dare someone kill her beloved mother!

The swelling rage invigorated her, motivating her to act. *What would Wilfred do next?*

A memory sparked from the day before. Visit the doctor who signed the death certificate.

Swinging her legs over the edge of her bed she went to the window and drank in the sweet country air. The comforting gurgle of the creek bounced its way up to her bedroom, helping to soothe her troubled soul.

Ophelia was already up, putting the kettle on the stove.

"We need to visit the doctor today," they both said together.

"Twin telepathy," said Ophelia placing two cups on the table. "We've still got it."

Imogen slid onto a chair.

"Do you remember when I pinched a gobstopper from the sweet shop while Mrs. Humby had her back turned?" asked Ophelia. "I swear that woman had eyes in the back of her head. She was about to grab my wrist and call me a thief when you pretended to faint. I was able to slip the stolen goodie into my sock while she was distracted. When she recovered and asked me to open my mouth and hands, my innocence was proven."

"I do," replied Imogen, chuckling. "And I felt guilty about it for months."

There was no doctor in the village. The closest was in the town of Parkford, about three miles north. It was the same doctor who had come to the fête and examined Willa's body.

"I'll race you to get ready after we eat!" said Ophelia. "And I'll call for a taxi."

Parkford was a medium-sized town, perched atop a hill that overlooked a valley. Most of the dwellings were newer, as were the businesses, constructed of red brick. The only history was in the very center of the town where a water pump and fountain marked the spot of the original post chaise stop. A white marble lion's mouth spewed water from the spring that had watered the horses and early villagers. The modern town had grown up in a web around it.

The doctor's surgery was in one such, no-nonsense, redbrick building along a wide street behind the fountain. It had a smart, shiny, black door and a brass knocker.

A woman in her fifties with tight, graying curls looked up over wire rimmed glasses as they entered, her eyes swinging from one twin to the other.

"How may I help you?" Her voice was unexpectedly whiny, and Imogen had to smother a laugh.

"We're here to see Dr. Pemberton," explained Ophelia.

The woman closed an eye. "I gathered that."

"Uh, of course." It was unusual for Ophelia to be cowed and Imogen wondered if it was part of her plan.

"Do you have an appointment?"

"No. Is that a problem?"

The receptionist cocked an eyebrow and flicked through her appointment book. "Which one of you will be seeing the doctor?"

Imogen caught her sister's eye and gave a slight nod.

"Me," said Ophelia. "My sister is here for moral support."

"Are you patients of Dr. Pemberton?"

"No."

"If you'll take a seat and fill out this form, the doctor can see you in ten minutes." She handed them a clipboard and pointed them to a waiting room where a young boy was holding his arm at an unnatural angle and sniffing. They assumed the flustered woman next to him was his mother since they shared the same shade of bright orange hair. An elderly gentleman whose hands were on top of a battered cane, eyes closed, sat on the other side of the room.

Ophelia began to fill out the form. "We're going to need a doctor at some time."

The receptionist called a name and the woman and boy stood as a young girl in her early twenties, exited the doctor's office.

"Ow!" The young boy's yelp bled through the door after a couple of minutes.

The waiting room was strictly business with hard wooden chairs and a couple of *Country Gentleman* magazines.

"You're humming, lovey," said Imogen.

"Am I? I tend to do that when I'm bored."

The elderly gentleman cracked open an eye and a hint of a smile pulled at his lips.

The doctor's door opened again to reveal the boy sporting a sling and red eyes. His sad gaze haunted them as his mother hurried him out the door.

The receptionist called another name and the old man rose unsteadily and shuffled into the doctor's office. As soon as he was gone, a younger man entered from the street and after checking in at the desk came to sit with them in the waiting area.

"Good day!" he said in a scratchy country accent.

"Good day!" they responded.

The young man's eyes were darting nervously. "Here to get my tonsils checked." His hand moved to his throat. "Might have to have surgery."

"Oh, it's nothing to worry about," said Imogen. "My grandson had his taken out a few years ago."

"I'd rather keep mine," the man responded. "God gave them to me for a reason."

How could one argue with that?

He picked up one of the magazines and started flipping pages without reading them.

The old man exited, wrinkled eyes moist.

"Next!" shouted the receptionist.

The twins stood and nodded to the young man before entering the doctor's office. It was full of heavy, good quality furniture and smelled of disinfectant. They remembered the square man with the shining, bald head. He smiled up at them with instant recognition as Ophelia handed him her form.

"You were at the village fête. Terrible tragedy. Now, what seems to be the problem, Miss Harrington?"

"Actually, I'm in fine health but we thought it prudent to register with you since we've recently moved back to Saffron Weald." She waited.

"Saffron Weald? Harrington? You must be related to Beatrice Harrington?"

"We're her daughters," responded Imogen. "We understand that you were her doctor, too."

"Indeed, I was. Lovely woman."

"We were hoping you could tell us more about her passing." announced Ophelia.

He smiled over the top of clasped hands. "Textbook. Died peacefully in her sleep."

"It was just so sudden," said Imogen.

"Well, she was ninety-five," he responded with raised brows.

"It's just that the last time we saw her, she seemed so healthy," persisted Imogen. "Had she been ill, at all? She didn't tell us, or we would have come to see her."

"No. Fit as a fiddle for someone her age. Her ticker was strong, too." He tilted his head. "But when it's your time, it's your time."

"You have no reason to believe she had struggled in the passing? We just hate to think of her making that final journey alone," Ophelia explained.

"I think I can set your minds at ease on that count. She had a cleaning lady, Mrs. Bumble or something, and it was she who found your mother. There was a teacup on the table by her bed and the cleaning lady just thought she had overslept. She went in to open up the curtains but your mother didn't move. Upon inspection, it was evident she was gone. The cleaner hurried down to call me and I arrived a few hours later. All was in order. Rigor had set in. I'd say she died shortly after going to bed."

"Was she on her back or curled up on her side?" asked Ophelia.

Imogen's heart caught in her chest.

Dr. Pemberton's expression changed. "I'm not sure what difference…I say, is there something you're not telling me?"

The sisters exchanged a look before Ophelia replied, "In going through our mother's things, we found evidence that she was worried for her life."

A kaleidoscope of emotions fanned across the doctor's face ending in a frown of concentration. "On her side. Legs tucked up."

"Mother always slept on her back," said Imogen, slapping the top of his desk. "In her youth, her mother was of the opinion that any other way of sleeping was unhealthy. Consequently, Mother always slept on her back."

"If someone had put something in her tea, say, some poison, would one curl up in pain?" asked Ophelia.

Dr. Pemberton's unremarkable eyes flared. "Yes. I would say so. But…I can't believe it. I had no reason to think…"

"If you were to review Mother's case now, through the lens that she had been poisoned, would you sign the death certificate differently?"

The doctor's hands went to his smooth chin as he considered. He closed his eyes.

"Given what you have told me, and upon reflection, I might have suspected foul play. But I had no grounds…" He took a deep breath. "Her face was somewhat strained but no more than others I have attended who have died in their sleep. And she was of advanced age." He winced as if in pain.

Ophelia flapped her hands. "We don't blame you at all, doctor. Be assured of that."

"It was such a cut and dried case," he moaned. "I was in and out in fifteen minutes."

"Please, don't blame yourself. I know Mother wouldn't," Imogen assured him.

"But who would want to kill a nice old lady?" he groaned.

"We believe Mother's death may be connected to the girl, Willa, who was killed at the fête. Mother was snooping about on behalf of the young girl, whose mother had died in Saffron Weald twenty years before."

The doctor's jaw dropped. "What?"

"We found correspondence from Willa among Mother's effects, concerning the disappearance."

The doctor's polished head dropped into his hands. "I may need to report this to the authorities."

"We thought you might," said Imogen. "And we have no objection. We're highly motivated to solve this puzzle."

"I'm sure the police are doing everything in their power," he blustered.

"But have they connected Willa's death to her mother's? And now *our* mother's?"

"Then you should take what you know to the police," he implored. "Not try to solve it yourselves. It could be dangerous."

"And do you think the police will take two old ladies seriously?" Ophelia asked.

Dr. Pemberton chewed his cheek.

"Exactly!" she responded. "Unless or until you can prove that Mother was murdered, we have to take things into our own hands."

# Chapter 20

Sitting side by side on the ragged, old furniture in the sitting room that evening, the sisters talked through the current state of their investigation.

"As long as we keep all this about Mother under our hat, I think we should be safe," Ophelia assured Imogen. "As far as the rest of the world is concerned, she died of old age. If we tell our suspicions to the police, as the doctor suggested, it will stir things up and spook the murderer. That could make us a target. Let the killer believe we don't know."

"What about the doctor?" asked Imogen. "He has to make some kind of report, he said."

"It will take some time for the wheels of government to roll, I believe. So we just need to speed things up."

"Alright," agreed Imogen. "And I have to tell you that something has shifted in me. I am so enraged that it's pushing me past my fears. But I do keep worrying that Mother suffered. Hasn't the discovery of her murder affected you at all?"

Ophelia's head reared back. "Of course! What do you think I am? An unfeeling machine? I'm torn up inside that someone had the temerity to kill Mother. To hurt her. But I'm channeling that anger into action. Let's find the scoundrel and bring them to justice." She made a bridge with her hands.

"I didn't mean to suggest…"

Ophelia waved her sister's apology away. "We're in unchartered territory here, ducky. We don't know how we're supposed to react. But let's have it unify not divide us, eh?"

Imogen nodded, grateful for her sister's wisdom.

"Now, I don't think the poison would have taken long to go into effect," Ophelia assured her. "I happen to know that cyanide, for example, kills within fifteen minutes."

Imogen's head jerked up. "How on earth do you know that?"

Ophelia blinked. "Chap in my building was in the police. He told me all about it."

"Sometimes I feel like I don't know you at all!" declared Imogen.

"Nonsense! You know me better than anyone." Moving over to the gramophone, Ophelia flipped through the jazz records that had arrived while they were visiting Dr. Pemberton in Parkford. "Who's left on our list that we haven't talked with yet?"

"Connie, Reginald and Mildred."

Ophelia huffed. "I wish Mildred was a little less zealous. She certainly gets the job done but I want to run a mile when I see her coming."

"I know what you mean. Let's leave her to the end."

"Well, we're in need of some more groceries since the garden is failing us, so tomorrow we can go to *Tumblethorn's* which will give us a chance to have a chin wag with Reggie. And we can use our book research as an excuse to drop by the library again and talk to Connie."

The mellow tones of the jazz slid into the room.

"Do you think Connie got rid of her dog?" asked Imogen.

"I jolly well hope so. If it's terrorizing her cat and wreaking havoc on the furniture, she should act quickly in case the farmer changes his mind about taking him back."

"Do you think her acquisition of the dog bodes well for her innocence?"

Pushing out her bottom lip, Ophelia considered the question. "I suppose so."

"I understand her fear. I don't feel quite at ease myself," opined Imogen. "Makes me really miss my Wilf."

"As I said, there are two of us and as long as we don't blurt out our suspicions and divulge that we think Mother was murdered, I don't see that we're in any real danger." Ophelia put a finger to her lips.

"You weren't particularly careful at the Puddingfield's," Imogen pointed out with a wry grin.

"It's a bit of a dance, ducky. We won't find out anything valuable if we stick entirely to small talk."

Imogen huffed then tilted her head. "What band is this? I rather like it."

"They're American. *Smokey Syncopation*."

"The lead singer has a mesmerizing voice," commented Imogen.

The shrill sound of the telephone interrupted their listening.

"I'll get it," said Imogen.

Ophelia could hear her muffled voices coming from the hall.

"That was Pierre," said Imogen. "He can bring the furniture tomorrow so that will change our plans a bit. He said the workers will be here around ten."

Ophelia put a palm to her forehead. "With everything that's happened, I'd completely forgotten about all that!"

The news of the imminent arrival of their new furniture was a bright spot that both sisters needed. And to think it had all belonged to a duchess!

After an early breakfast, the sisters dusted and swept to prepare their nest and at ten o'clock sharp, there was a knock at the door.

"Come in!" said Ophelia as Imogen watched from the hall.

A youngish, brick of a man, dressed in a brown duster, swiped off his hat. "Mike Palmer. I understand you need your old stuff moved out too."

"Yes, come this way. Living room first, I think."

Mr. Palmer followed, then let out a large sigh.

"Is something wrong?" asked Imogen.

"That door is rather narrow. Not sure we can fit the new sofa through it. Let me get a measuring tape. I'll be right back."

"Oh, dear! I had rather set my sights on the duchess's cast-offs," groaned Imogen.

"Don't be faint of heart," reprimanded Ophelia, swishing around the room as if she were the duchess herself. "Have faith."

Mr. Palmer returned with his yard stick and measured the width of the door. "It'll be tight, but we'll give it a go." He disappeared again.

Imogen clasped her hands under her chin and stepped out into the hall. "I'm trying to be optimistic."

Mr. Palmer returned at one end of the big sofa and a young man of about fifteen staggered under the weight at the other end. When they reached the living room door, Imogen held her breath.

"Not much room to turn in," said Mr. Palmer, ducking in the low hall. "Bob, go left."

The young man swung round but hit the side of the hall.

"That's as far as I can go, Mike."

Michael Palmer hoisted the heavy sofa onto his shoulder and bent his knees, inching through the doorframe. "It's stuck! Try pushing from your end, Bob."

"Yoohoo!"

*Mildred!* Imogen rolled her eyes and dug down deep for patience.

"What have we here?" sang Mildred examining the dilemma. "I had the same problem in my cottage. Just needs a good thump." She put her considerable weight behind the couch and pushed hard. It popped through.

"There!" Mildred dusted off her hands.

"That's the biggest piece," shouted Mr. Palmer, "so I think we shouldn't have a problem with the rest."

Imogen eyed the twisty stairs and wondered.

"Thank you," she said to Mildred. "I thought we might have to exchange it and I had my heart set on that particular piece."

"You're very welcome. Now, I've come to ask for your help with W.I. business but I can see that you're busy, so I'll come back another time. Tata!"

As she was leaving, Pierre walked through the front door.

"Chérie!" he said, kissing Imogen on both cheeks. "I 'ave come to check that all is well."

"It almost wasn't," she admitted. "But Mildred dealt with the problem."

He dropped his voice and winked. "Then she is good for something."

Imogen swiped him on the arm.

They walked into the living room as Mr. Palmer and Bob were coming out with the old sofa. "Sir."

"I had them put it right where the other one was," said Ophelia, leaning to kiss Pierre. "Or should we be wild and shake things up?"

The elegance of the fabric and the curve of the carved wood highlighted the shabbiness of the rest of the room.

"It makes more sense to 'ave it facing the fireplace so you can put the two armchairs on either side," said Pierre, gesturing with his hand. "The room is not large and does not offer too many other variations, I think."

"Brilliant suggestion!" beamed Ophelia and Imogen had the strange feeling of being extraneous again.

"Coming through!" Mr. Palmer and Bob each had an armchair on their shoulders that they shifted to their arms as they came through the door. "Where to for these?"

"Let's put them either side of the fire," Imogen said.

As the moving men removed the old chairs, and shifted the sofa into its new location, the duchess's furniture endowed the room with a more elegant feel. Imogen flopped into one of the armchairs which melded to her shape.

"Luxurious!" she cried, in a voice as duchess-like as she could manage.

The rest of the furniture exchange had not gone without problems. As Imogen had surmised, the steep, twisting stairs made hefting the bed frames up and down, something of a challenge, but eventually it was all in.

"Now we must get some food or it will be bread and jam for dinner," declared Ophelia after Pierre left.

As the bell to the grocer's tinkled, Reggie swept through the beaded curtain. Today he was wearing a ruffled purple shirt with yellow braces which he snapped with his thumbs.

"How lovely! What can I do for you? I have a smashing batch of cucumber jam, just in." His expectation of their pleasure at the news was written all over his pliable features.

Ophelia decided not to look at her sister for fear that her expression would betray her opinion on the topic of cucumber jam.

"We're in the line for staples today, Reggie."

"Then I'll let you shop. Give me a hoot when you're ready. Mother and I are enjoying a program on the wireless."

Once their baskets were full, they rang the little bell on the countertop and Reggie reappeared.

"How are you feeling about the murder?" he asked in a gossipy tone of voice. "Have to admit, it has me spooked. You were there when Connie found her if my sources are to be believed. Good job Mother and I have Mr. Tibbles for company."

"That is correct, but we've been a bit too busy to dwell on it," lied Imogen handing over the items from her basket.

"From what I've heard, it seems she was a stranger using a false name." He added the price of the items on a pad of paper next to the cash register. "Can't imagine why?"

"Hmm," said Ophelia as non-committally as she could.

"And I heard she was from Wiltshire, of all places," he continued.

"Is that so?" began Ophelia. "Have *you* ever been to Wiltshire, Reggie? I've heard it's very nice."

Reggie lifted his head in thought. "I think we made a school trip there once to see the chalk horses. I wasn't overly impressed."

He picked up more of their items and continued his calculations.

"Did you hear we're undertaking a history of the village?" asked Imogen.

Reggie looked up. "Wasn't your mother doing something like that?"

*Had she told everyone her secret?*

"Was she?" responded Ophelia. "She didn't tell us."

"Yes, the last time she came to see Mother, she mentioned it."

"How did she seem, Reggie? I worry that she wasn't well before she died and didn't tell us," said Ophelia.

"Oh, no! You shouldn't worry about that," he said, adding up the total. "That will be five shillings, please."

Imogen opened her purse and counted out the money.

"Fit as a flea, Mrs. Harrington was. She had a spring in her step and a twinkle in her eye. In fact, I was complimenting her on how well she looked, the day before she died. It was the same with my father, you know. He was laughing and joking in the evening and by the next morning he was gone. Nothing we could have done. Nothing." He looked over their heads into space.

"What year was that?" asked Ophelia.

"1922. Mother still hasn't recovered, poor thing."

"Anyway, we thought now is as good a time as ever to get started on our little history project. We found mention of the colonel's military promotion in a history book and did you know that one of the inhabitants from years ago was secretary to the Prime Minister."

"Archibald Newcome!" said Reggie. "We learned about that in school, too. Our teacher was related to him. Find any other nuggets?"

"Just something about an unidentified body that was found up near the hall."

Reggie stopped still. "A body? Did it say who it was?"

"No. We just saw it in the book. It was ruled an accident anyway. It was around 1908, I think."

Reggie paled.

"Coming Mother! See you soon ladies. Tata!" He disappeared through the beaded screen.

As the sisters made it out to the pavement, Ophelia said, "I didn't hear Mrs. Tumblethorn, did you?"

"No. I think he made it up as an excuse to stop our conversation. Now why would he do that?"

# Chapter 21

"Well, the bodies are piling up but we're no further forward in finding out who the murderer is," commented Imogen, trying to relax in one of the duchess's luxurious armchairs.

"I disagree," said Ophelia. "We've discovered several people who have a connection to Wiltshire. We know that the vicar lived in the village next door to Willa's mother, that Reginald has been to Wiltshire at least once and that the mention of Willa's mother's body sent him scurrying. We know that the Puddingfields had a son in Wiltshire—"

"We need to look at a map to see how far those places are from West Wallop."

"Splendid idea. The library should have those."

"Then we can chat with Connie too."

"Getting back to what I was saying," Ophelia gave her sister the evil eye. "We've now discovered that three people here have a connection to Wiltshire."

"I see what you're saying but does it take us further forward, lovey?"

Ophelia tapped her chin. "I wish I'd been able to remove those notes Willa made about the newspaper stories. But that would have been pushing our luck."

"We could always go to Salisbury and look at the archived articles ourselves."

"Of course! Sometimes you have the odd, brilliant idea, ducky."

Imogen bristled.

"That came out wrong," Ophelia hastened to add.

A knock on the door interrupted her apology.

"Well, it can't be Connie or Mildred. They just barge in." Ophelia pushed herself up and went to answer the door returning with a middle-aged man in a rumpled brown suit and matching hat with a testy expression.

"This is Inspector Southam," Ophelia said, making her eyes wide behind his back. "He has a few questions."

Imogen's heart plummeted off a cliff.

"Do have a seat, Inspector," she managed to say. "Can we offer you some tea?"

He sat down, took out a thick notebook and thumbed through it with stubby fingers. He was a nailbiter.

"No, thank you. Look, I'll get straight to the point. I've made several visits to West Wallop in connection with the murder of Willa Medford."

Imogen bit her lip.

"Would you mind telling me what the two of you were doing in her house a few days ago?"

Imogen watched as her sister's mind worked overtime. "How did you know?"

"I'm sure I don't have to tell you that identical twins make quite an impression. When I went back to question the neighbor a second time, she asked after my 'assistants'." His brows rose.

Ophelia's hope that he would put the neighbor's strange report down to the fanciful ravings of an old woman had not come to pass. "Ah, yes. Well, we found a letter from Willa Medford to my mother. She recently died and we were going through her things. It made us curious."

The inspector's face hardened and he slapped a palm on the arm of the duchess's chair. "Why didn't you come forward? This is the kind of information that could help us solve the case. Do you still have them?"

"We do," said Imogen, creeping to the desk like an ashamed dog to retrieve both letters. She handed them to the inspector and the room fell silent but for the accusatory ticking of the grandfather clock.

"This confirms what the information at Miss Medford's house indicated. It seems that Willa was sure her mother had been murdered on a visit to Saffron Weald."

"Yes," agreed Ophelia. "And our mother died between Willa's letters which is why she didn't respond the second time. Willa had no way of knowing that. The fête gave her an excuse to come in person."

The inspector tutted while shaking his head. "This is why amateurs should leave the policework to us. Instead, they poke their noses in and get themselves killed." He looked up and pointed with his pencil. "That includes you two."

Imogen ducked her head in shame, but Ophelia held the inspector's gaze. "Do you have any information on her mother's demise?" Ophelia wished she could read his small mind.

His thick brows met in the middle as he sized them up. "Do you?" It was like a standoff at the O.K. Corral.

"We know that a woman who looked like Willa, came to Saffron Weald twenty years ago and never returned. We also know that an unidentified woman was found two months after her disappearance."

The inspector made a grumbling sound. "*If* the unidentified woman found in 1908 was, in fact, Willa Medford's mother, the death was ruled an accident. Only the recent murder of Willa connects the two deaths and calls that conclusion into question. I have seen the old police report *and* the death certificate. The doctor concluded that the woman had fallen down the embankment and knocked her head on a large rock that was bloodied. The body was not discovered for two months, by which time a certain…degradation had occurred." His eyes narrowed. "The young viscount was informed of the incident. He was in Scotland at the time of her death and asked the police to keep the discovery quiet as he was about to make an advantageous marriage and did not want any gossip connecting him with the tragedy, to derail the arrangement. The police honored his wishes but kept the case open for six months. No one came forward to report a missing person."

Ophelia's mind was working double time. How much should she reveal to the inspector? "I would hazard to guess that the grandmother was frightened for the child and didn't report her daughter's disappearance for fear of the murderer coming after them."

"Sounds about right," agreed the inspector. "So, now we have a string of three murders. Numbers two and three covering up the original killing, as I am sure you know from reading the confidential diaries." He glared at them through bushy eyebrows.

"Yes, and we did see in the journal entries that the first victim was found in a well. Do you know anything more about him?" asked Imogen.

The inspector pushed his top lip up to his nose and rustled the pages of his notebook. "Albert Houndstooth. By all accounts a distinctly eccentric fellow. Unmarried. Lived alone. A mad scientist of sorts. Had all manner of chemical equipment in his barn. But I can see why his death was ruled an accident. If not for the other two killings, I might not be convinced it was murder myself."

"I've forgotten the description of the stranger Willa's mother met," said Ophelia, shooting an arrow into the dark.

Glancing at his notes, he murmured, "Short, dark bearded man with a scratchy voice. Not much to go on."

"Ah, yes. I remember now," Ophelia lied.

The inspector cleared his throat. "Now, I should report you two to the commissioner for impersonating police officers—"

Imogen gripped her pearls.

"—but I don't think that will be necessary *if* you promise not to do it again." His caterpillar brow wriggled.

Ophelia sent a warning message to her sister to be quiet. "Of course! So very kind of you Inspector Southam. We're just a couple of silly old ladies looking for adventure."

"Well, this kind of adventure might get you killed," he snapped.

"We'll stick to our latest hobby of writing a history of the village," said Imogen.

"See that you do!" said the inspector in a parting shot.

"Let me show you out." Ophelia led the inspector from the room and down the hall. Imogen joined her at the door as they watched him leave.

"Should we have told him about Mother?"

"Absolutely not! I found his attitude insulting and condescending. I mean to find her murderer before he does."

## Chapter 22

Ophelia spent the morning practicing the violin. It was a particularly difficult piece by Mendelssohn, and she attacked it with vigor, appearing in the kitchen flushed red as a ripe tomato.

"I've made you some tea," announced Imogen. "I'm thirsty just listening to you." She slid a teacup across the table. "And I made Mother's coffee cake." She took a bite and wrinkled her nose. "Not as good as Mother's. I'll have to practice."

She opened their ratty old notebook that sat beside the gold spiraled one. "I added the information on the stranger in West Wallop to our notes."

"You seem less agitated by it all today," said Ophelia breaking off a piece of the cake.

"I had a talk with Wilf last night—"

Ophelia's face burst into astonishment mixed with skepticism.

"—I don't mean his ghost came to me or anything, but I still like to talk things over with him."

"Alright…"

"Anyway, someone needs to be held accountable for Mother. She was a lovely person who never hurt anyone and I'm outraged that a murderer robbed us of her before her time. My anger is chasing away my fear."

"Glad to hear it!" responded Ophelia. "I thought the shock of the inspector calling us out would have the opposite effect, to be honest."

"Well, he did make me nervous, and he could have reported us for housebreaking, but he didn't. So, I'm not going to cry over what-ifs."

"Excellent!" Ophelia popped the morsel of cake into her mouth. "It's good!" After chewing for a minute, she continued. "I lay awake thinking last night, too. The inspector said Willa's mother described the stranger as a male. That takes all the women off our suspect list. Furthermore, the man was short and bearded. Now, it's easy enough to shave off a beard but you can't disguise your height."

Imogen clapped her hands. "So, the colonel is out and Pierre. That's a relief!"

"And the vicar," pointed out Ophelia. "But it leaves Reggie, Archie and Harold."

"I wish I knew what spooked Reggie so much the other day. Now he's like a tortoise in a shell. I doubt he'll talk to us because of whatever we said that rattled him."

"We were talking about the unidentified body in the woods," mused Ophelia. "The report said Willa's mother had been dead at least two months. I wonder who found it?"

Imogen flicked through the transcribed coded notes of her mother to the page about Reggie. "Mother says he is a birdwatcher."

Ophelia thumped the table. "He would have been in his early twenties in 1908. What if *he* discovered the body while bird watching but didn't tell anyone. He's unconventional, but he's also a bit of a wimp. I can see him being terrified and running home to his mother. It didn't matter in the end because the body was eventually found and never identified. But I would imagine us mentioning it could stir up old guilt."

"Do you know, I think you may be on to something. How can we validate this without a direct approach?"

"We could talk to his mother, old Mrs. Tumblethorn. She's got to be in her eighties now and appears to be homebound. If we could find out when Reggie goes on his birdwatching rambles we could stop by for a little chat." The clock showed the time to be just on noon. "However, I've been thinking. We should pay Mrs. Bumble a visit, first. I had quite forgotten she found Mother, until the doctor mentioned it. I want to hear *all* the details now that we know her passing was not natural."

Mrs. Bumble, cleaning lady, lived in a row of tiny, stone cottages in Norbridge, the next village over. As she came to her sunny, yellow door, she gasped, stubby hand pressed to the front of her full length, floral apron.

"Well, if it isn't the Harrington twins! To what do I owe this pleasure? Are you wanting some help with cleaning? Come in, come in!"

She hurried them into a cozy living room, pictures of children on every available surface.

"Actually, we've come to ask you about finding mother," explained Imogen, settling herself onto a stiff sofa. "We were too preoccupied to ask at the funeral but now that the dust has settled, we wanted to know some of the details."

"Of course, you do!" responded the woman who reminded Ophelia of one of the nesting Russian dolls she had seen in a shop in Dorking. "What do you want to know?"

"Can you walk us through how you found her?" prompted Ophelia, feeling the prod of a spring in the seat of her armchair.

"I cleaned for your mother Mondays and Thursdays, arriving at ten and leaving at two. Mrs. Harrington always made me a nice lunch. Anyway, that morning, when I arrived, she wasn't at the kitchen table as she usually was, but at ninety-five I thought maybe she'd had a restless night. So, I popped up the stairs and knocked ever so gently. When she didn't reply, I walked into the room to check she was alright. She was curled up in bed, so I thought I'd leave her be, but something seemed…off. It was too quiet, you know. So, I went over to the bed. Now, I've seen my share of the departed and I could see right away that she was gone." She clasped her hands on her knee.

"I hurried downstairs to call Constable Hargrove, who said he'd call the county doctor and then be right over. Not ten minutes later, those lovely ladies from the Women's Institute arrived.

"I was in a bit of a daze, so I let them fuss around me. One of them made me a cup of tea and sat me in the living room. But it was that nasty stuff your mother kept for the colonel.

"When the constable arrived, he asked me a lot of questions while the ladies tidied up the kitchen. About an hour later the doctor came, examined your mother then wrote out the death certificate. He put the cause as, 'death incident to old age'. I know because I asked him.

"Then the W.I. ladies prepared her body for the undertakers. They were so kind."

"Had she seemed well the last time you saw her?" asked Imogen.

"Oh, yes! But what better way to go? Some old folks decline slowly, ending up bedridden or gaga. Your mother was one of the lucky ones."

After a little shopping and small talk in the high street, it was Pierre who informed them that the birdwatchers club met on Wednesday afternoons when the shops had a half day. Being that it was Wednesday, they returned home to prepare another of their mother's coffee cakes, and walked around to the back entrance of *Tumblethorn's Grocers*.

The back door was open. "Cooee!" called Imogen. "Mrs. Tumblethorn!"

"In here!" squeaked a frail and broken-down voice.

They wandered through a storage area then found a side room, staged as a comfortable living-cum-bedroom. Upon a rocking chair, sat an unnerving relic of the past wearing an old-fashioned Victorian dress and widow's mob cap, fragile as a pressed flower that has lain undisturbed for fifty years. Mrs. Tumblethorn had once been a vigorous woman in her forties back when the twins left Saffron Weald, and the drastic alteration in her constitution made them falter.

She had been widowed twenty years before and had allowed her husband's death to trigger the beginning of her own, leaning into the grief, letting it rob her of the life she had left. Homebound, not by her health but by her preference, she had shrunk into little more than a living skeleton with sunken eyes and bony fingers.

The twins glanced at each other, and Imogen gulped.

"Come in, my dears," the widow insisted. "I don't get many visitors." She let her gaze travel from twin to twin. "You look just like your mother."

The air reeked of grizzled skin and Imogen had to take out her lavender-soaked handkerchief and press it to her nose. Ophelia opted for an armchair close to the old lady, and Imogen, a chair from the little table.

"That's why we came," said Ophelia. "We know that you and mother were friends and it felt like the right thing to do now that we have taken over possession of the cottage."

"Bea was a good friend to me," she croaked. "Between Reggie and Bea, I knew everything that was going on in the outside world."

They let her ask questions about Imogen's family, first.

"I don't know how you can carry on as normal after losing your husband," Mrs. Tumblethorn said. "I admire your courage. I lost the will to go forward. If it wasn't for Reggie, I'd have died long ago."

Next, she peppered Ophelia with questions about her musical career.

"Your mother would pop over when she'd been to one of your concerts. She'd bring a record of the symphony and play it for me—after she described the theater and the gowns the women wore. It was such a treat."

"Would you like a piece of her cake? We used her recipe," asked Imogen who was holding the cake on her knee. She could not be sure that Mrs. Tumblethorn still ate.

"Ooh! Yes, please," she cackled. "Put the kettle on and we'll have tea." A small stove sat in a corner.

"So, Reggie is a birdwatcher," said Ophelia, stating the obvious.

"Oh, yes. Done it since he was a boy. He makes drawings of them too. He's very talented." She pointed to a sideboard. "Open that door, dear. That's where he keeps his sketch books."

While Imogen fiddled with the tea things, Ophelia withdrew the sketch book feeling a little as if she were going through someone's underwear.

"Won't Reggie mind?" she asked.

"No! He's actually quite proud of them. Though shy." She winked a crepey eyelid. "With my encouragement, he's entered a few into art shows and won some ribbons."

Ophelia opened the cover and gasped as she beheld a colorful wood warbler that was so vivid it seemed to jump off the page. She half expected it to sing.

"I had no idea," she declared. She looked at the date. April 1922. The next page held a chaffinch. Reggie had captured the tilted head that looked so much like concentration. "You say he's done this since he was a teenager?"

"Oh, yes. He has stacks of these books in his room upstairs."

"He should sell them. Has he shown them to Pierre?"

"They're like his babies. He couldn't let any of them go. It took all my strength to get him to enter them into the art contests. Plus, he doesn't want others to criticize them."

Ophelia could understand that. John Q Public often felt it his duty to criticize his fellow beings. That had been true of the orchestra, perhaps even more so since theirs was an all-female one. You had to learn to develop a thick skin.

"Is his early stuff as good as this or has he improved?" she asked.

"He's definitely improved but he's always had an extraordinary flare for it. Don't know where he got it. Neither his father nor I were artistic in any way."

Mrs. Tumblethorn lifted a paper-thin hand to her mouth and coughed. Imogen handed her a cup of tea, watching its progress as it wobbled its way to the side table.

"It's wonderful he maintains an interest in something he did as a boy," Imogen remarked, cutting a thin piece of the coffee cake and laying it on the occasional table next to the teacup.

"Every week, like clockwork." She stopped and looked up at the ceiling. "Well, almost every week."

The hair on Ophelia's neck stood on end. "What happened to stop him?"

The old lady became serious, her wrinkled lips wrapping around almost toothless gums. "It was a bad time for us. My husband had died, and Reggie was finding solace in the forest until…" her rheumy eyes snapped up. "…he fell over a dead body."

Imogen inhaled sharply and Ophelia warned her to stay quiet with a look a librarian might give a noisy patron.

Ophelia returned her gaze to the whisper of a woman and waited.

"It was 1908. I remember it so well because of my husband's passing. Reggie tripped, thinking it was a tree root, but when he opened his eyes he was face to face with a young woman who was definitely dead. She'd been dead for some time and the insects, well, you know.

"The poor boy lost his stomach contents then ran home as fast as he could. He was shaking and jabbering so much he wasn't making any sense. But I knew he'd had some kind of shock. Wouldn't talk about it for days. When Reggie finally told me, he begged me not to make him go to the police for fear they would make him go back.

"I was lost in my own grief and didn't press him. Then a month later, my sister told me about the Stirling's steward finding a body on the estate. She was the housekeeper up there, back then. Lord Stirling swore them all to secrecy. It seems he also asked the police to keep the discovery quiet as he was about to marry a very wealthy woman and didn't want any bad publicity. As I understand it, no one came forward to claim the body and after six months the case was closed. It was ruled an unfortunate accident, anyway. Took Reggie a whole year to get up the courage to go back."

# Chapter 23

Having decided to research the original death, the twin sisters were back at the train station on their way to Salisbury. This time they each purchased a first-class ticket and were the only ones waiting on the platform. The weather looked more stable than on their last jaunt, but they took their brollies anyway.

Under the warmth of the summer sun, they walked into Salisbury in search of the county archives. The city center was a complete hodge podge of architecture including classic Elizabethan, and they felt at least a little gratitude for the way their own tyrannical historical society made the village cling staunchly to its heritage.

Walking under a pretty arched bridge that joined buildings on two sides of the street and reminded them of Oxford, they approached a solid, Greek revival municipal building that housed the archives.

At the imposing information desk, they explained what they needed to a highly fashionable flapper, who directed them to a corridor in the east wing.

The wing happened to be badly lit and poorly ventilated and Imogen tugged at her high collar. Sturdy tables for research filled the room, headed by another information desk. This time the clerk was anywhere from forty to sixty, dressed in tweed from head to foot with a severe bun and wire spectacles.

"Good afternoon," began Imogen. "We are interested in archived county newspapers for the year 1907."

The woman grunted as she scribbled down the information and scurried away returning two minutes later with a box labeled '1907'.

The county paper was a weekly circular. Fifty-two copies were stacked in the box.

"I suppose we should start with January," said Ophelia, reaching into the box for the top paper. Imogen lifted out the February edition.

By the time they reached the June and July papers, their eyes were suffering from the strain and their noses, from the frowsty air. They had found nothing.

"I think we should reward ourselves with a nice cream tea after this," declared Imogen as she reached for August and handed Ophelia the September edition. "Hard things are always easier when there's a sweet reward at the conclusion."

Ophelia muttered and opened the first page with a frown.

Two minutes in she shrieked, "Bingo!" The other researchers shot them dirty looks.

She began to read quietly,

*"Albert Houndstooth of West Wallop, age seventy-three has been declared missing since he missed a dental appointment on August 30$^{th}$. When he failed to arrive at a scheduled meeting with his solicitor the following week, the solicitor, a Mr. S. Poole, reported the fact to the police. A search of the premises did not find Mr. Houndstooth and circumstances in his cottage suggested that he had not left for a holiday. Police undertook a large-scale search of the village and surrounding areas to no avail. Anyone with information on the disappearance of Mr. Houndstooth is asked to contact Salisbury police."*

"Now we need the 1908 papers."

Ophelia scribbled down the facts while Imogen went back to the po-faced clerk to ask for the next year.

"Willa's mother said the body was discovered about a year after Albert went missing so I'm going to begin with the August edition." She handed Ophelia the September one.

Half an hour later, they reached for the October and November papers.

This time it was Imogen who shot her fist in the air and with a stage whisper cried, "Hurrah!"

*"After the disappearance of Albert Houndstooth, a distant relative who claimed the property, hired workmen to fix the well, whereupon the body of Albert Houndstooth was found at the bottom. Decomposition had reduced Mr. Houndstooth to a skeleton but he was identified by his father's watch and a gold tooth. The police were called and after extensive investigation, the death was ruled an accident as some of the bricks from the top of the well had come loose and were under the body.*

*As well as being a retired schoolteacher, Albert Houndstooth was an amateur chemist as were his father and grandfather before him.*

"Just as Willa's mother said," said Ophelia. "But *she* didn't believe it was an accident."

"And paid for her suspicions with her life," declared Imogen.

When the sisters exited the county archives, the weather was still fine and after asking for directions, they headed for the nearest tea shop.

"Miss Harrington? Mrs. Pettigrew? Fancy 'meating' you here!" Harold Cleaver clomped across the square toward them. He was dressed in dark trousers and a jacket, with a flat cap. "Been to the live animal auction."

"So far from home?" commented Ophelia.

"I go to the auctions in four counties. That's why my meat is the finest at the best price. What are *you* doing here?"

They explained they had an interest in the cathedral and wanted a day out.

"We're headed for some tea. Would you like to join us?" Imogen asked him.

"Don't 'teas' me," he chuckled. "Don't mind if I do."

Once they had ordered, Ophelia began her interrogation since Harold was on their short list.

"How long have you been coming to the auction in Wiltshire?"

He pushed his jaw out, making his lips bunch. "Thirty years, must be."

"That long?"

"Where else do you go?" asked Imogen.

"Dorset, Berkshire, and of course, Hampshire. Harriet runs the shop for me on market day."

"Do you come by train?" Imogen continued.

"Only if my car has a flat tire, which seems to happen quite a bit." His laugh was like the bellow of one of the bulls he purchased. "Makes a nice day out and breaks up the monotony of working in the shop."

Imogen took off her gloves. "Doesn't Harriet ever come with you?"

"She doesn't like to travel, on the whole. She comes once a year on Mayday when Salisbury has their maypole celebrations. They put on quite a show. We close the shop and make a day of it."

The teas, scones and cream were delivered by a nervous looking waitress.

"I love everything about cows," declared Harold rubbing his meaty hands together and ladling thick cream onto his scone. "From the butter to the cream to the beef and the hide. One of God's greatest gifts to man, if you ask me."

He was the epitome of a jolly butcher.

"Are the auctions friendly?" asked Imogen as she tried to eat her scone without the jam spilling off onto her plate.

"Not always," he admitted. "There are times when a truly spectacular cow comes along. I can tell just by looking at her she'll have a superior flavor. But if *I* can, so can the other chaps. It's got a bit tense a few times, but nothing a good beer in the pub after can't settle."

"Do you ever venture out into the surrounding villages?" asked Ophelia as she poured the tea.

"Why ever would I do that? Don't know anyone there. Much rather take a load off in the pub with my friends."

"Of course." She offered him the sugar bowl. "We used to have an old friend from here. What was his name Imogen?" She snapped her fingers as she pretended to think.

"Oh, you mean Burt?"

"That's him! Albert Houndstooth. Don't suppose you ever bumped into him?"

Harold flipped up the peak of his cap and scratched his curly head. "Can't say as I have, no. Is he a butcher?"

"No," she responded. "He's a teacher. Never mind. You never know."

"Have another scone, Harold," said Imogen, pointing to the plate.

They were lucky enough to find a compartment to themselves on the ride back after saying farewell to Harold Cleaver who was headed to the pub.

"Although he claimed not to know Albert, Harold is a regular in Wiltshire, and has been for thirty years. *And* he's not too tall. I'm afraid he's still checking all the boxes for our murderer," decried Imogen, clearly distressed by the fact.

"He's also handy with a knife," said Ophelia with a grin. "He's covered in blood every day, so I don't suppose he'd be squeamish about escalating to a person."

"Ophelia!" cried Imogen. "Let's not stoop to being crass." She pulled off her gloves and set them on her lap. It was uncomfortably warm in the compartment. "I simply cannot imagine our friendly butcher hurting a fly."

"But I believe murder is an outlier," contradicted Ophelia. "Career criminals are just nasty pieces of work, out to steal what they will not earn for themselves and generally, create anarchy. Murder is different. It's usually committed to solve a problem."

"Even so."

Ophelia stared out the window at the meadows. "I know. But *someone* did it."

"I keep thinking that if we had arrived at the supply tent ten minutes earlier to get the rope, we might have caught the murderer red-handed or better still, prevented Willa's death altogether," sighed Imogen.

"Yes, the killer took quite a chance. Which points to desperation."

"Oh," said Imogen like a trombone sliding down the scale. "That's another box Harold crosses off—he was on the fête committee. He had both the means and the opportunity to kill poor Willa."

"There is one thing in his favor though," said Ophelia. "Unless he sprinkled arsenic on Mother's sausages and she ate them for supper instead of breakfast, I don't see how he could have killed her at night."

"Oh, good thinking," said Imogen checking her appearance in a compact mirror. "And Mother *never* ate sausages for supper. I'm glad, Harold is far too nice to go to prison."

"Umm. If we figure this out, the murderer will end up with four deaths on their slate."

Imogen tucked some hair up with a pin. "True. Which reminds me, we haven't spoken to Mildred yet. We've been putting it off."

"Well, since we now know the killer is male, we only need to pump her for random information on the other suspects. Ooh. I've had a thought—if we go to *her* house we can leave when we want."

"Splendid idea. I think we'll have to make another one of Mother's coffee cakes. By the time we're done, mine will be as good as Mother's!"

# Chapter 24

Mildred's cottage was much smaller than Badger's Hollow. Its exterior possessed the black and white plaster and timbers, but its thatched roof was in serious need of a trim and the window frames were thirsting for attention. Furthermore, instead of being set on an acre, it was in the exact center of a much smaller plot of land.

Ophelia had suggested they give Mildred a taste of her own medicine and arrive unannounced. Imogen knocked on the flaky, bird's-egg blue door. After a few minutes, Mildred answered. She wore a pinny around her generous waist, a rather unbecoming skirt and blouse and her fine hair was full of static.

"Oh!" she exclaimed, her voice full of regret as she tried to flatten her unruly mop. "How lovely."

Ophelia produced the coffee cake. "We wanted to thank you for the warm welcome."

Mildred's eyes brightened. "I shouldn't—but I will." She flattened herself against the wall to let them pass by.

The door to the living room was open and Mildred ran to close it but not before Ophelia caught a glimpse of a room in total disarray. Was Mildred spring cleaning in July? They followed her into a snug kitchen piled high with old newspapers, dirty dishes in the sink and unfolded washing on the table. Mildred scooped the washing off and popped the pile into a wicker basket.

You could have knocked Imogen over with a feather. She had imagined an orderly house to match the meticulously efficient person who owned it. This was pure and utter chaos.

Mildred moved over to a pile of unanswered correspondence sitting on one of the chairs, whisked it away and invited Ophelia to sit. Then she gathered up a stack of newspapers from another chair to make space for Imogen.

"Have you heard anything more about the murder?" asked Mildred casting an anxious eye on the various piles.

"Why do you think *we* would know?" asked Ophelia sweetly, placing the coffee cake in the center of the table.

Mildred took a dirty knife from the sink and wiped it on her apron before cutting three large slices of cake. "Well, a little bird told me that the inspector came to see you."

"He didn't come to see you?" asked Ophelia.

"No. Wish he had. I expect it's because you two found the body." She took a bite and chewed. "Well?"

Ophelia quickly filed through the information that she thought would be common knowledge. "Miss Medford had come to Saffron Weald because she was hoping to find out information about the disappearance of her mother."

"Yes, I already know that," said Mildred dismissively. "The police believe the girl's mother was the unidentified body that was found twenty years ago in Stirling Woods." She swatted the air sending cake crumbs flying. "Can't believe they kept *that* under wraps all these years. Even *I* knew nothing about it. And the police have the nerve to say we're all treated equally under the law."

Imogen realized she was referring to the influence Lord Stirling had exerted to keep the discovery of the body quiet.

"What on earth was the girl's mother doing all the way from Wiltshire in an out of the way place like Saffron Weald?" Mildred twisted her lips and her eyes narrowed to slits. "I bet there was some funny business with him up at the manor house which would explain the need for secrecy."

"Oh, no!" said Imogen in Mrs. Medford's defense. "There was no suspicion of anything like that. She'd just had a baby."

"But wasn't she a widow?" challenged Mildred. "Or so she *said*. What if there was no dead husband and the baby was really Lord Stirling's? No wonder he wanted to keep it a confidential matter before his marriage!"

Ophelia felt a film of filth drape over her. "Such a thing has *never* been suggested, Mildred. I think we could do better than defame a woman long dead. As I see it, there's no reason to believe that Mrs. Medford was here for any nefarious reason. I think the police would have told us because it would be pertinent to her daughter's murder."

Mildred cut another slice and tucked into it. "But it does bear considering. If the girl who died at the fête *was* Lord Stirling's natural daughter, she might have come asking him for money. He could have arranged to meet her in the supply tent, then killed her to get rid of the sticky problem before his wife found out."

"That is *not* on the inspector's mind at all!" cried Imogen, aggravation tracking all over her. "I think you'd better keep that opinion to yourself, Mildred. From what we hear, Willa and her mother were very respectable people."

Mildred harrumphed while cutting a third slice of cake. "But you never know, do you?"

Ophelia felt her skin prickle with irritation. "Did Willa interview you at the fête?" She was highly motivated to steer the thorny conversation in another direction.

"Yes, she did. Seemed like a nice enough girl but then she turned out to be a blatant liar. It really is quite distressing."

"If you thought your mother had been murdered and the case was twenty years old and the police no longer had an interest, you might do the same thing, Mildred," retorted Imogen, her hackles rising again.

Mildred put a palm to her chest, gathering up her most pious expression. "I would *never* lie. Honesty is always the best policy."

"But Willa knew she was looking for someone dangerous. Someone who had already killed three times."

Imogen realized her mistake. "I mean twice." She caught her sister's eye.

"You don't remember her mother coming to the village in 1908?" asked Ophelia quickly to cover the error.

Mildred laid down the piece of cake she was holding. "No. I've struggled to think about it and I do not remember any such person. Wish I did, then I'd have some useful information for the police. I suppose she *had* to have been in Saffron Weald since her body was found here."

"Perhaps you were busy back then," suggested Imogen noticing the dust balls under the table.

Mildred's lips flattened. "I was thirty in 1908. Mother and Father were still alive but in poor health. Yes, I was probably consumed with their care." She remembered the cake.

"Oh, well. Have you persuaded Pierre to join the bell ringers?" asked Ophelia.

"He says he doesn't have the time," Mildred replied. "Have you considered it?"

"I'm still trying to adjust to a completely new life, Mildred. I would hate to commit to something and not be able to keep my promise."

"Well, that's true. We can't have someone who isn't dependable."

Imogen saw her sister's shoulders flinch.

"Can we count on you for tonight's performance?" continued Mildred.

"Remind me what it is again?" asked Ophelia, flashing her gaze at an equally confused Imogen.

"*Lady Hayward's Experiment*," replied Mildred. "It's a comedy. It's really quite funny."

"Oh, yes, of course!" responded Ophelia. "We'll be there. What time does it start?"

By the time Imogen and Ophelia arrived at the village hall that evening, the only seats left were in the back. Malcolm Cleaver handed them a program, dressed in full livery.

They were sitting next to Rosalind Bloomfield, the florist.

"Not an actress, Miss Bloomfield?" asked Imogen.

"I was busy enough with the planning for the fête," she exclaimed as the lights went down.

Many of the prominent members of the community had a role in the play and for once, Mildred had not exaggerated, it was a delightfully funny comedy providing a much needed escape from the stress of sleuthing.

Just before the intermission, a new character entered the stage who seemed familiar though neither of the twins could immediately place them. Imogen looked in the program and pointed with her finger, then whispered to Ophelia, "It's Connie, dressed as a gentleman."

Even with this knowledge it was difficult to recognize her, wearing a brown suit, reddish mustache and beard with matching wig and a felt hat. Walking with a heavy step, she produced a tolerable tenor voice.

"They must have run out of male actors," concluded Ophelia as the curtains closed. "Which is often the case in a small village, I suppose. I must say, it actually adds to the comedy for me."

Alice Puddingfield was selling homemade lemonade at the refreshment table. "How do you like it so far?" she asked them.

"Pleasantly surprised," said Ophelia. "We live among talented people, it would seem."

"I bet they'll try a musical now you've moved back," replied Alice as she handed out cups of the yellow beverage.

"They'd better wait about six months before asking me," warned Ophelia.

"What about you, Imogen?" asked Alice.

Imogen's mouth pulled down. "Oh, no. I don't like being in the limelight, but I could help backstage."

"Well, they always need help with that," Alice responded.

The lights flickered. Time to get back.

Malcolm Cleaver played his part as a footman extremely well and the happy ending, that was a surprise to no one, resulted in roars of delight from the eager audience. Imogen's hands ached from clapping as the actors took their bows.

Pierre found them after. "What did you think? This was even better than the usual offering."

Ophelia's smile was different. "Delightful!"

"Splendid!" responded Imogen. "Do you act, Pierre?"

He shook his head pushing his monocle into his breast pocket. "Not if I can help it."

"Perhaps you just need the right persuasion," said Ophelia in a husky voice.

# Chapter 25

Pushing through the old library door, the twins headed over to Connie. She was looking much better, in spite of her late night at the theater.

"Hello," she said. "What did you think of last night's production?"

"Fabulous!" said Ophelia. "Took us a while to recognize you, though."

Patting the air with her hands she explained, "They had too many women try out and not enough men, as usual, so I said I'd take a small man's part. I've done it loads of times before. Shakespeare used men as women since it was not deemed genteel for women to be on the stage back then. If it was good enough for him, it's alright by me."

"You were splendid," said Imogen. "But didn't it make your throat hurt?"

"Nothing that a drink of hot lemon and honey couldn't cure," responded Connie.

"Did you return Tiny yet?" asked Ophelia.

"I'm taking him back to the farm on Saturday. The RSPCA called to tell me they just had a springer spaniel brought in. It belonged to an old lady who died, over near Byminster. I know I said a spaniel wasn't big enough, but Tiny has cured me of that idea. At least a spaniel will warn me of danger by barking." She glanced at the time. "Actually, could you do me a favor? I have a publisher's rep coming in to try and sell me books, in half an hour. I don't suppose you could go over, when you're done here, and let Tiny out for a minute or two? I'm not going to get a lunch break today."

"Of course," said Ophelia.

"There's a key under the flowerpot on the front step. Now, I'd better get on before the rep arrives."

She shoo shooed them away and they returned to the history section and began to scour the shelves for more books on local history.

Imogen stopped at a guide to ancient churches in the south of England. Flicking through, she soon found their own proud church. It described the architecture in detail and had some black and white photographs. In one of the pictures, the photographer had accidentally caught the profile of a woman walking through the churchyard, on the edge of the picture. She squinted but it didn't help and went back to the desk to ask if Connie had a magnifying glass.

Moving over to a window for better light, she held the glass above the picture. Magnified, she could see that the woman had turned just as the photograph had been taken. She started, shook her head to clear it, and looked again.

Finding Ophelia in the stacks, she handed her the book and the magnifier without saying a word but indicating the page with her eyes.

Ophelia squinted then looked up, astonished.

"It's Willa's mother!" she whispered tightly. She turned to the front of the book to find the year it had been published. 1908! She closed the front cover to discover the author. David Clark. "There must be a thousand David Clarks in England alone," she thought. Then she had an idea. She opened the fly leaf again and searched for the name of the photographer. The room began to spin. *Thomas Harrington.*

"What's wrong?" asked Imogen. Ophelia merely pointed.

Imogen's head snapped up. "Daddy?" She took a deep breath. "He did get one of the first Brownie cameras, I recall. It was one of his hobbies. And he was still alive in 1908. How extraordinary!"

"But don't you see? Both Mother and Father crossed paths with the blighted Mrs. Medford. It's like a sign, ducky. If I had any doubts about solving Mother's murder before, they've vanished. It's as if they've reached back through the veil to communicate with us."

"I know!" Imogen examined the page. "Who's the publisher? Perhaps they will have an address for this David Clark."

"Let's check the book out so we can take it home."

They wandered over to Connie's desk in a daze.

"Card?" she asked.

"We don't have one yet," replied Ophelia.

Connie frowned and glanced at the clock again. "The publisher's rep will be here any minute and I need you to let Tiny out. Take the book but fill out the form soon. I don't have time right now."

Three small peaks defined Connie's pretty cottage. The flower beds were weed free but some of the flowers were laying on top of the soil, gasping for water. Deep, brown holes dotted the front lawn like unsightly blemishes. The path was made of cobblestones and the twins picked their way across, being careful not to roll their ankles.

A giant, bass bark rumbled through their ribcages before they even made it to the porch.

"Do you think he's friendly?" piped Ophelia.

"Only one way to find out." Imogen reached under the flowerpot and pulled out the key as the sound of snuffling noises made their way outside. Pushing open the yellow front door, a flash of black and brown fur lunged, knocking Imogen off kilter so that she lost her balance. She fell off the step and into Ophelia's arms. A large, pink tongue slobbered all over her chin.

"Hello boy!" she crooned, righting herself and running her hands over the smooth fur between his ears. "He's excessively friendly!"

Ophelia, stiff as a board, stood rooted to the ground. "He's enormous!"

"He's a teddy bear," crooned Imogen. "Let's see if we can find him a toy."

She leaned in and found a red ball in a basket. She and her sister swapped places, Ophelia clung to the door frame in terror, while Imogen threw the ball and began a long game of fetch.

"I don't think he'll ever tire of this, but I have," declared Imogen. "Come on, boy. Let's get you a drink." She patted her thighs and the giant fur ball trotted over, tongue lolling out of his mouth, past Ophelia and into the kitchen.

They followed. It was a neat little room but the flagstone floor was scattered with hundreds of multi-colored sequins. Imogen reached down to rescue the remnants of one of Reggie's ill-conceived, sequined hot water bottle covers. She wagged her finger at his nose. "Bad boy!" Tiny hung his head.

Finding a stoneware bowl on the floor, she filled it with water and he began lapping as if he had not drunk in several days, water flying all over the stone floor.

"We should take a look around," said Ophelia eyeing the dog with suspicion.

"Do you think that is quite proper, lovey?" asked Imogen. "It seems like a betrayal of trust. Besides, I thought we had narrowed it down to men?"

"Maybe there were two people involved. This is too good an opportunity to overlook. A gift-horse, so to speak."

Imogen grumbled her disapproval.

"May I remind you that *someone* killed mother! The rules are different now, ducky. Not to mention, Connie invited us in."

Imogen wrinkled her nose. "Well, it feels wrong to me."

"Alright, you clean up the mess and watch the dog and I'll do the snooping. Warn me if anyone comes."

Ophelia started up the stairs and came out onto a tight landing that presented three doors. The first was a pocket-sized bathroom. She looked in the cupboard on the wall above the bath. There were cleaning things, some lavender bath salts and some kind of glue.

The next door was obviously Connie's bedroom. The walls, rug and bedding were all light pink. Ophelia shuddered. She went to the chest of drawers and opened each one. The top had underwear that one would expect for women of a certain age. The next was full of white nightdresses neatly ironed and folded. The bottom drawer contained handmade sweaters in various variations of pastel. On the table by the bed stood a little lamp and a dish of sweets.

A dressing table displayed mother of pearl inlaid brushes, face cream and hair pins. She moved on to the wardrobe but found nothing but skirts and dresses for every season with shoes in neat rows at the bottom.

Creeping out, she opened the third door. The boxy room was messy compared to the rest of the house and looked like a storage room. Old, dusty hobby horses leaned against the wall and a doll's house that was missing the roof sat on a table. A portable clothing rack held a man's suit like the one Connie had worn for the play and old-fashioned ball gowns. A battered dressing table with a mottled mirror sat on one side of the room. Opening one of the drawers she found a false brown beard, and wig. A smaller drawer revealed a dried up tube of actor's gum.

Descending, Ophelia moved into the living room. Its walls displayed the timbers that made up the outside walls and heavy floral curtains hung to the floor. An occasional table by a delicate armchair held another dish of sweets and a book. Connie's desk sat by the window giving her a lovely view of the front garden.

Ophelia sat at the desk which was spic and span as a new penny. Each drawer was neatly organized with correspondence and receipts. She was hardly surprised that there was no smoking gun.

She returned to the kitchen where the enormous dog was napping at Imogen's feet.

"I just think Connie's not a dog person. He's so gentle." Imogen looked up. "Find anything?"

"No. Not that I really expected to."

"Come on, then. We've done what she asked." Imogen pulled the book about churches out of her bag. "We've got more important things to see to."

# Chapter 26

There was no telephone number listed for the publisher in the front of the book, so Ophelia called the telephone exchange.

"Bosworth and Sons Publisher," sang a young female voice, once Ophelia was put through. "How may I help you?"

"I'm interested in contacting one of your authors," began Ophelia.

"Please hold while I transfer you."

"Hello." It was a refined male voice.

"Good afternoon. I have in my possession a book about ancient churches of the British Isles and was interested in contacting the author." She gave the book title and the author's name.

"I hope you understand that we keep our author's private details confidential," the man replied.

"Of course! I was hoping you could get a message to him for me? Or perhaps he has an 'in care of' address."

"I'll have to look it up in our index. Please hold."

She tapped the wall while she waited. Imogen sat on the bottom stair anxiously listening to one side of the conversation.

"He's going to their index of books," Ophelia explained.

"I wonder how many books they've published? I've never heard of them."

"Me neither," agreed Ophelia. "Frankly, we're lucky they're still in business." A crackle on the other end indicated the young man's return.

"Let's see. It's an old book. David Clark. Yes, there is a solicitor's address."

"That will do nicely."

Ophelia wrote the number and address down on a notepad. "Thank you so much for your help."

She hung up and gave the number the publisher had given, to the girl at the exchange.

"Westlake, Westlake and Westlake Solicitors." The accent was Cornish.

Ophelia asked to speak to the oldest Westlake.

"I'm sorry but he has retired. I'll put you through to his son."

"Hello?" The deep voice was not unfriendly.

Ophelia explained why she was calling.

There was a pause at the other end of the line. "Twenty years ago, you say? I'm sure he was a client of my father's. Can you hold while I check?"

"Of course."

She began to drum the wall again as Imogen pummeled a handkerchief.

"Hello? Yes, I did find a file for David Clark. I hope you appreciate the fact that I cannot give out his number since he employed us as an intermediary." Ophelia's hopes slumped. "But I can give him *your* number. Then the ball will be in his court, so to speak."

"Splendid!" Ophelia hung up after reciting their telephone number. "Well, we've done what we can," she explained to Imogen. "Now all we can do is wait."

Peter Cleaver, painter and decorator, arrived with color samples. After deciding what shades to repaint the various rooms, and plying him with tea and cake, the phone rang.

"I'll get it," said Imogen as she closed the front door behind the young worker. "Saffron Weald 259, Imogen Pettigrew speaking."

"This is David Clark. My solicitor said you were interested in contacting me." The voice was crisp and educated with a slight wheeze that indicated he was a pipe or cigarette smoker.

Imogen's stomach clenched with excitement. "Yes! Thank you so much for calling. We found your book in our local library and were pleased to see an entry about our church in Saffron Weald in your collection. It was a long time ago, but I wonder if you remember anything about your visit here?"

A sharp noise indicated doubt. "I published that book twenty years ago. I'm afraid I don't remember much about it at all."

"The reason we are so interested is that my father, Thomas Harrington, is listed as the photographer—"

"Oh, wait! Yes, I *do* remember that now. My blasted camera had packed up and I was swearing and blasting in the churchyard when your father approached to ask what was wrong. When I explained, he said he was somewhat of an amateur photographer and could run home to get his camera, which he did. Since he'd shown an angry stranger such kindness, I invited him to take the shots and told him I'd give him credit in the finished book."

"What a fascinating story! You can't imagine how happy it made us to see his name cited in the book," gushed Imogen. "He's been gone for many years now."

Ophelia had wandered into the hall to listen and Imogen flapped her hands to indicate that it was David Clark.

"I'd be happy to send you a signed copy for your own personal collection, if you'd like," said Mr. Clark.

"Wonderful! How kind." She gave him their address.

"Was there anything else?" asked the author.

"Actually, there is one more thing," she paused. "In one of the pictures taken in the churchyard, the photograph captured the edge of a profile of a young woman. I don't suppose you remember anything about her?"

A moment of silence made her wonder if he had hung up, but no dial tone sounded. "Sorry, I'm racking my brain. I have a slight recollection that she asked me about the village but when I explained that I was a visitor we parted company. Do you know her?"

"No," replied Imogen. "But I do happen to know she was killed shortly after that picture was taken."

Since David Clark was going to send them their own copy, the sisters decided to return the book to the library and fill out the forms for their own library cards. Connie was not at the desk but the assistant librarian, the niece of Mildred's, was in her place.

"We need to fill out the forms to apply for a library card," they explained to the sunny girl with red hair and matching freckles.

"Welcome! I've heard so much about you already," she beamed. "How fun to come back home." She handed them the forms. "You can find a table in the children's section. Here's some pencils."

They returned a few minutes later with their completed forms, and as the assistant librarian was creating their cards, Connie appeared.

"Thanks for letting Tiny out yesterday. How did it go?"

"He's lovely!" declared Imogen. "He was so excited to see us."

Connies' eyebrows flickered. "Lovely maybe, but destructive. Did you see what he did to my new hot water bottle cover?"

"We did, but he's just restless. You're probably right about your place being too small. He needs to burn off energy roaming around the farm."

"Just two more days. I'm more than ready. Look, could you do me another favor and let him out again? I can't leave for lunch, I have too much to do here."

"We'd be delighted," replied Imogen. Ophelia groaned.

As Imogen opened Connie's front door, no dog greeted them. She frowned. "That's odd!"

No sooner were the words out of her mouth than Tiny appeared at the top of the stairs, panting. "There you are!" However, instead of bounding down the steps to greet them, he turned tail and went back into one of the upstairs rooms.

"Oh, dear! I'd better go and see what he's got into," Imogen tutted.

She stepped over a chair which had been laid on its side to prevent Tiny going up the stairs.

Following the sounds of scratching, she entered the storage room. Tiny was working away at a loose floorboard with his claws.

"Stop it, boy!" commanded Imogen, but the dog ignored her. She moved forward to grab his collar and stood between the dog and the floorboard. Crouching down to push the board back into place, she caught sight of the edge of a hidden wooden box. The dog placed his snout on her shoulder.

"Ophelia! He's found something."

Her sister appeared in the doorway. "What?"

Imogen reached into the hole in the floor and withdrew an intricately carved box with a small lock.

Ophelia's eyes widened and she took a pin from her hair. "Here." Imogen handed her the box.

Within seconds, she had cracked the lock to reveal a cache of legal documents.

"*Flaming fiddles!* There's a letter from a solicitor in Wiltshire…" She dropped her arms and looked up at her sister. "It's concerning a suit brought against the Featherstone's by none other than…Albert Houndstooth."

"That's too great a coincidence! What kind of suit?" asked Imogen, keeping the energetic dog at bay.

Ophelia scanned the document. "It's about the lining of rubber boots. He claims to have proof that Horace Featherstone—who I assume to be Connie's grandfather—stole his father's idea for the cotton linings." She read on. "He claims the two men met at a tavern in Salisbury one day and hit it off because they were both interested in science and inventions. Mr. Houndstooth mentioned that he was working on a way to make rubber boots warmer for farmers but had not cracked a formula that made it easy to paint the cotton onto the rubber interior. They parted company and then not a year later, Mr. Featherstone was credited with the invention and made a tidy sum on the patent of the idea. The older Mr. Houndstooth died shortly after this and never mentioned the incident to his son. But in going through his father's things, many years later, the son, also a hobby scientist, found an entry in his father's diary. This prompted him to search through his father's old scientific journals where he found the record for the idea, dated *five* years before Mr. Featherstone's patent."

Imogen sank onto a rickety chair. Images of boots, sequins, sweets and false beards swam around in her head. "When is the letter dated?"

"April 1907," replied Ophelia.

Imogen sat up sharply. "I know what happened."

# Chapter 27

An owl hooted.

Huddled together beneath the broad oaks at the back of the church, Pierre, Imogen and Ophelia waited nervously. Steadily falling rain made for a gloomy and decidedly damp summer evening. The twins crowded under one dripping umbrella while Pierre stood under his own.

Time slowed, almost coming to a standstill.

Imogen fingered her locket and checked her watch for the fifteenth time. "Perhaps the ruse didn't work."

"Patience, ducky. Patience."

"I would 'ave expected Ophelia to be the impatient one," chuckled Pierre.

Once the sisters knew Pierre was not the murderer, they had laid out their theory, and the plans to catch the murderer, in order to ask for his help. As daring as they were, at their age, they accepted that it would not be wise to confront a serial murderer alone. Arms folded, legs outstretched as he listened, Pierre had applauded when they were done and immediately agreed to be part of the plan.

The owl hooted again and the pre-arranged time for the rendezvous came and went.

"Perhaps I got it all wrong," whispered Imogen.

"I doubt criminals are the best timekeepers," Pierre assured her, but even before he finished speaking, a shadow began to cross the graveyard, in a jerky fashion. The meeting place had been the back porch of the church but instead of stopping, the figure jerked on, making a beeline for them under the old trees.

"*Hot crumpets!*" gasped Imogen in a strangled whisper. "That rather complicates things."

"Don't worry. I'll take it from here," hissed Ophelia. "Tiny!" she called out loud, as the dog burst upon them and nuzzled into Imogen's legs.

"Oh!" cried Connie, a bag swinging from her arm. "What are you three doing here?" She turned her head around like the owl searching for his next mouse.

"We might ask you the same thing?" responded Ophelia.

"Me? I'm just taking Tiny for a walk. You were the ones who suggested burning off some of his energy."

"Are you expecting someone?" persisted Ophelia as Connie's head continued to scan the area.

"No! What made you think that?" Connie tugged on Tiny's lead.

"It's just that we bumped into Mrs. Bumble. You remember her? Mother's cleaning lady."

Even in the soggy darkness, the whites of Connie's eyes shone bright through the thick lenses. "Mrs. Bumble? Oh, yes. What was she doing in Saffron Weald this late?"

"She told us she was meeting you but that something had come up and she had to leave. We assured her we'd let you know."

A million decisions fired behind Connie's scared eyes. "I had no plans to meet anyone. She's talking nonsense. I don't even know the woman. I'm just taking Tiny for a walk."

"That's funny because Mrs. Bumble mentioned that Willa Medford had sent her a letter."

Connie tossed her head but said nothing, trying to control the dog.

"Mrs. Bumble also divulged that she had made arrangements to give that letter to you. I told her we could pass it along."

Connie took on the look of a rabbit caught in a trap. Tiny was pushing his snout into Imogen's hand asking for her to pat his head. Connie yanked on his lead again with no effect.

"Uh, a letter, you say? Do you have it?"

Ophelia began to pat the pockets of her mackintosh, then to search in her handbag. "It's here somewhere…"

Connie began pacing on the spot.

"So, you *did* set up a meeting with Mrs. Bumble?" needled Pierre.

Connie's bottom lip pulled down, eyes fixated on Ophelia's hands. "It slipped my mind."

Ophelia prolonged the imaginary search for another three minutes, causing Connie to resemble a steam engine ready to blow. "Do you have it or not?" she screeched.

Pierre turned on a torch.

"Ah, here it is." Ophelia handed Connie the letter without an envelope, the official letterhead of Albert Houndstooth's solicitor, plain to see, even in the dim light of the torch.

Connie flinched as if Ophelia were handing her a cobra and dropped her grip on Tiny's lead. Imogen reached for it and Tiny came to stand beside her.

"What is this?" Connie's voice was shattering.

"This is actually the letter that got this whole mess started over twenty years ago," explained Ophelia as the rain beat its rhythm on their umbrellas. "Tiny found it."

If Connie's eyes could shoot flames, they would have instantly incinerated the Alsatian. "Stupid dog!"

"When we discovered your grandfather had made a small fortune designing a warm cotton layer for rubber boots, you forgot to mention that he *stole* the idea from someone."

"That is a *lie!*" howled Connie. "Grandad thought of it, created it and patented it."

"If that is true, why did you disguise yourself as a bearded man, travel to West Wallop and push Albert Houndstooth down his own well after receiving this letter?"

Connie clammed up.

"Unfortunately, when you arrived in West Wallop you had to ask someone the way to Albert's small farm. I'd place good money on the theory that person happened to be Willa Medford's mother. You must have slipped up and mentioned you were a visitor from Saffron Weald. But you thought it wouldn't matter, because the woman would remember you as a man, a part you had perfected over your years in amateur theater productions. And I suspect you destroyed any other legal documents you could find in Albert's home concerning the matter.

"However, a year later, his relative began work on the well and Albert's body was discovered. When the police ruled it an accident, you thought you were in the clear, but something bothered Willa's mother. She remembered the stranger who had asked the way to his house around the time the police thought Albert had died. No one would listen, so she took it upon herself to do a little sleuthing. She came to Saffron Weald, not once but twice. When you saw her the second time it must have alarmed you, and somehow you arranged to meet her in the woods on Stirling land. Then, you either pushed her down the embankment or smashed her on the head with the rock and she fell."

Ophelia paused but Connie remained mute, her jaw taut as a drum.

"The problem had been resolved. And for twenty years you got away with it and lived your life feeling that even though you couldn't get your family's money back, you had saved your grandfather's reputation from ruin."

A growl emanated from Connie's throat, rain dripping from her hood.

"Then Willa's grandmother died, and she discovered that the story she had been told about her mother's death was a pack of lies. She couldn't rest, and finding *our* mother's name among *her* mother's notes, she wrote a letter. Mother must have mentioned it in passing, either at the library or perhaps the Women's Institute. It was like a ghost rising from the dead that would not die. You *had* to stop Mother talking about it. So, you poisoned her." Ophelia's tone became dangerous. "How *dare* you kill our angel mother!"

This time, Connie cowered.

Pierre choked. They had withheld this information from him the night before.

Ophelia took a moment to compose herself and Connie twitched as if she were going to make a run for it. Pierre stepped forward and she thought better of it.

"Then Willa showed up at the fête," continued Ophelia. "I assume you recognized her straightaway, even though the girl was using a false name, because she was the image of her mother. I doubt one easily forgets the faces of those you murder." She waited a beat. "You panicked. I don't know how you lured Willa to the supply tent, but you managed it and whacked the poor girl on the head. I suspect, after killing three people, you were pretty hardened. So much so, that you had the temerity to show up in the tea tent as if nothing was wrong. I remember thinking you looked flushed, but I put it down to helping to run the fête and the warm weather."

Ophelia made a guttural noise of contempt. "You knew full well what Imogen and I would find in the supply tent, so you offered to help us—I daresay it was to solidify your innocence. *We* were your alibi." Ophelia made a threatening gesture. "You are a despicable human being who deserves to hang!"

Connie's face was strained but at this accusation she straightened her shoulders. "You have no proof."

From out of the shadows, Inspector Southam stepped forward.

Connie jumped back.

"Actually, your appearance here tonight is tantamount to a confession, Miss Featherstone," declared the inspector. "You believed Mrs. Bumble had evidence that pointed to you as the murderer and that she was going to blackmail you." He nodded to the cloth carrier. "What's in your bag?"

Connie pulled it tightly into her chest. "It's private property."

Pierre and the inspector rushed to grab Connie's arms causing the bag to fall to the wet ground.

Ophelia opened it and withdrew a heavy, bronze statue.

"Looks like a murder weapon to me," announced the inspector, reaching for his handcuffs.

He cautioned Connie who was yelling and struggling the whole time, then frog marched her into a waiting car.

Tiny watched intently but did not attempt to leave Imogen's side. "I'm glad that's over," she sighed, her whole body sagging with relief.

Pierre spun around to face them. "Why didn't you tell me she killed your mother?"

"I wasn't ready," explained Ophelia as they watched the police car pull away.

"'Ow did she do it?" he persisted.

"Mrs. Bumble found Mother," began Imogen. "There was a cup of tea by her bed. Mother always took a cup up with her. When we first moved into the cottage, there was no regular tea in the tin, only the Darjeeling stuff. For a fleeting moment I thought it odd, but then forgot all about it.

"But, when we went to talk to Mrs. Bumble, she told us that the ladies from the Women's Institute had arrived to help, even before Constable Hargrove, and had busied themselves with tidying and the dishes. She also mentioned that Connie brought her a cup of tea but that it was 'that nasty black stuff' she kept for the colonel.

"Once we knew the murderer was Connie, it was easy to deduce that she had come over as early as she could after the news of Mother's passing, to throw the poisoned tea away before anyone else drank any, and to wash up Mother's cup."

"It's a good job Mrs. Bumble didn't make herself a cup when she first arrived," commented Ophelia.

"Well," said Pierre, "'ats off to you ladies."

"It was all Imogen," admitted Ophelia. "She's the one who had the epiphany after we found the solicitor's letter from Albert. It was all there, hiding in plain sight, but it needed someone intelligent to put it all together."

"Actually, Tiny was the key," said Imogen stroking his wet head. "Without his interference we would never have discovered the letter. Once we found it, I remembered the sequin and a crushed boiled sweet at the murder scene, among the other clues. At the time, I thought they could have been there for hours before the murder with so many people going in and out of the tent, so I didn't really focus on them. And back then, we had no idea that Connie had purchased one of Reggie's ridiculous hot water bottle covers. But the first time we went to let Tiny out, he had torn it to shreds, scattering sequins everywhere. Then, there were boiled sweets all over Connie's house in little dishes, and the storage room had a man's suit and a dark beard and wig. It was as though my brain shook it all out showing me that every clue pointed to the murderer being Connie."

"That's as fine a piece of detecting as I 'ave ever seen," said Pierre.

Imogen felt warmth in her cheeks.

"What are we still doing out here in the rain?" asked Ophelia. "Pierre, come and have tea with us to warm up."

"Only if you can guarantee it's not poisoned," he grinned.

# Chapter 28

Relaxing together with a glass of wine instead of tea, and Tiny curled up on Imogen's feet, Pierre complained, "I'm still 'urt that you didn't tell me about your dear mother?"

"It's been a hard pill to swallow," replied Ophelia.

"I should think so! 'Ow on earth did you figure out 'er death was not natural?"

Ophelia told him about the discovery of their mother's notebook with its haunting warning and their subsequent visit to Dr. Pemberton.

"She actually feared for her life? I wonder what 'appened?" mused Pierre.

"I suppose we'll never know. Perhaps that wasn't the first attempt Connie had made." Imogen shuddered. "It takes a real monster to murder a kind old lady. The only solace is that we have now caught her."

"Will there be an exhumation?" asked Pierre. "It's such a drastic step."

"The doctor is filing his report, and we shall see," said Ophelia. "Honestly, if they can convict Connie without having to resort to that, I will be happy. It seems such a desecration to disturb the dead."

"I agree," said Pierre.

The dog made a little grunt of contentment. "And what are you going to do about the dog?" asked Pierre.

"Farmer Tidwell is expecting him back tomorrow because he was too much for Connie to handle," began Ophelia.

"Oh! But Tiny helped solve Mother's murder," Imogen cried. "We can't send him away!"

"But we agreed, no pets, ducky."

"That's before we learned that mother was killed. Without Tiny, I'm not sure we would have figured it all out." Imogen rubbed behind the dog's ears and he smiled up at her with doting eyes. "He belongs here."

Ophelia rolled her eyes and Pierre shook his head.

"It's a lot for two ladies to take on," said Pierre.

"Two *old* ladies you mean," said Ophelia.

"But look, he's putty in my hands," Imogen pointed out. "He can sense I'm a dog person. He behaves far better for me than he did for Connie."

"That is true," said Ophelia eyeing the huge hound. "And no one would mess with us if he's around."

Imogen could feel the tide of opinion turning. "We have a fence, and a young gardener who will surely play with Tiny to get his energy out. I bet Malcolm would walk the dog too, if we paid him. And he's so cuddly."

Ophelia sighed in defeat. "I will agree, but these are my terms. He will stay with us for a probationary period. If, during that time, he is any trouble, I will take him back to the farmer myself." She placed her glass on the occasional table. "And I refuse to call him Tiny," she said with finality. "It's a ridiculous name for such a large dog."

"I doubt that dogs really speak English. 'E probably responds to the 't' and 'i' sound," said Pierre. "And perhaps the 'e' at the end."

"True," agreed Imogen. "Ti—, Tiber—Tiger!" The dog perked up.

"Oh, that's much more appropriate!" declared Ophelia.

"And 'e won't know the difference," Pierre assured them.

"That's settled then," said Imogen.

As if he understood, Tiger sat up and placed his huge, hairy head on Imogen's lap. She grabbed him behind the ears and crushed her face into his. "You're staying, boy," she whispered.

The dog sighed in contentment.

"Do you think Connie will be convicted?" asked Pierre.

"Oh, yes! There's far too much evidence against her. Plus, the inspector was right; her coming to the assignation was like a confession. Not to mention, she came prepared to murder poor old Mrs. Bumble. Connie is a lunatic!"

Pierre swirled the liquid in his glass. "How exactly did you get the inspector to fall in with your plan?"

"At first he was very angry that we were still meddling," said Imogen. "But when we told him about the solicitor's letter that set the whole thing in motion, and our theory that Connie had disguised herself as a man to travel to West Wallop to kill Albert, he was convinced. She told us herself she often took male roles in the dramatic society when the need arose."

"We called him after we set up plans for the trap with you," added Ophelia. "It was he who suggested keeping his presence a secret."

"And it seemed prudent to have a policeman as a witness," commented Imogen. "Furthermore, if things went sideways, we had more people to defend us."

"You could 'ave told *me* 'e would be there," said Pierre.

"We couldn't risk you looking for him and tipping Connie off."

"Ophelia! You know I would never do that!" he cried.

Ophelia's features adopted a unique expression, like she was warning him to be quiet.

Imogen wagged her finger between the two of them. "What *is* this? Why would *she* know you would not give the game away?"

He pursed his lips. "No reason. I 'ope *you* would know it too, Imogen. I'm not an idiot." He tipped his glass up and emptied it. "Anyone want more?"

"Not for me," said Imogen, watching the pair carefully.

"I'll have a little more," said Ophelia.

"And that's another thing," said Imogen, suddenly. "Who taught you to pick a lock, Ophelia? And don't give me that guff about locking yourself out of your flat."

Though she could not swear to it, she thought Pierre glanced at her sister.

"I told you, there was a policeman in my building. He helped me break into my own place several times."

"Hummph." Imogen was convinced there was more to it.

Pierre returned and filled Ophelia's glass. "When are you going to play your violin for the village?"

"Perhaps I'll put on a concert at Christmas," said Ophelia with a smile.

He winked. "I shall look forward to it."

# The End

*Thanks for buying my book!*

*Ann Sutton*

I hope you enjoyed book 1, *Village Fetes Can Be Murder* which is part of a new cozy mystery series I recently created, wrote and published.  In case this is the first book you have read of my works I also have two other cozy mystery series I have written that I think you will enjoy – The Dodo Dorchester Mysteries and the Percy Pontefract Mysteries.

The Dodo Dorchester Mysteries is currently an 11-book series.  Book *1* of that series, *Murder at Farrington Hall* is available on Amazon at a special introductory price.

https://amzn.to/31WujyS

*"Dodo is invited to a weekend party at Farrington Hall. She and her sister are plunged into sleuthing when a murder occurs. Can she solve the crime before Scotland Yard's finest?"*

If you would like a **free** prequel to the Dodo Dorchester Mystery series go to https://dl.bookfunnel.com/997vvive24 to download *Mystery at the Derby*?

The Percy Pontefract Mysteries is currently a 2 book series with book 1, *Death at a Christmas Party: A 1920's Cozy Mystery,* available on Amazon.

https://amzn.to/3Qb4BhG

***A merry Christmas party with old friends. A dead body in the kitchen. A reluctant heroine. Sounds like a recipe for a jolly festive murder mystery!***

"It is 1928 and a group of old friends gather for their annual Christmas party. The food, drink and goodwill flow, and everyone has a rollicking good time.

*When the call of nature forces the accident-prone Percy Pontefract up, in the middle of the night, she realizes she is in need of a little midnight snack and wanders into the kitchen. But she gets more than she bargained for when she trips over a dead body.*

*Ordered to remain in the house by the grumpy inspector sent to investigate the case, Percy stumbles upon facts about her friends that shake her to the core and cause her to suspect more than one of them of the dastardly deed.*

*Finally permitted to go home, Percy tells her trusty cook all the awful details. Rather than sympathize, the cook encourages her to do some investigating of her own. After all, who knows these people better than Percy? Reluctant at first, Percy begins poking into her friends' lives, discovering they all harbor dark secrets. However, none seem connected to the murder…at first glance.*

*Will Percy put herself and her children in danger before she can solve the case that has the police stumped?"*

For more information about all my cozy mystery series go to my website at www.annsuttonauthor.com and subscribe to my newsletter to see what I am currently working on.

You can also follow me on Facebook at:
https://www.facebook.com/annsuttonauthor

# About the Author

Agatha Christie plunged me into the fabulous world of reading when I was 10. I was never the same. I read every one of her books I could lay my hands on. Mysteries remain my favorite genre to this day - so it was only natural that I would eventually write my own.

Born and raised in England, writing fiction about my homeland keeps me connected.

After finishing my degree in French and Education and raising my family, writing has become a favorite hobby.

I hope that Dame Agatha would enjoy the Saffron Weald Mystery series as much as I do.

# Acknowledgements

I would like to thank all those who read my books, write reviews and provide suggestions as you continue to inspire.

*My proof-reader – Tami Stewart*

The mother of a large and growing family who reads like the wind with an eagle eye. Thank you for finding little errors that have been missed.

*My cheerleader, marketer and IT guy – Todd Matern*

A lot of the time during the marketing side of being an author I am running around with my hair on fire. Todd is the yin to my yang. He calms me down and takes over when I am yelling at the computer.

*My beta readers – Francesca Matern, Stina Van Cott*

Your reactions to my characters and plot are invaluable.

*20BooksTo50K* for their support of all indie authors and their invaluable knowledge of the indie publishing world.

Printed in Great Britain
by Amazon